STRUGGLE AT SOLTUNA

Struggle
at Soltuna

KARIN ANCKARSVÄRD

Translated from the Swedish by Annabelle MacMillan

Illustrated by Fermin Rocker

HARCOURT, BRACE & WORLD, INC., NEW YORK

Contents

5

STRUGGLE AT SOLTUNA

1

In the Rowboat

THE lake wasn't so large that you couldn't go from its northern tip to its southern bank in little more than an hour by rowing briskly. Rowing across it took half an hour. Jon and Rickard had timed it both ways. Their advanced standing as pupils in the Soltuna Consolidated Latin School had made them interested in numbers and calculations.

For the most part, the land surrounding the lake was the domain of plants and animals and, to a small extent since the beginning of the twentieth century, of mankind. The woods literally imprisoned the water. Hills and cliffs covered with dwarf pine trees provided the only visual relief, with here and there a marshy meadow giving way to reeds.

From the middle of the lake, you could see only two or three structures that betrayed the presence of human life. One of them was the summer cottage belonging to Dr. Halvorsson, Jon's father—Sand Cape, it was called, because it fronted on the only stretch of sandy beach along the lake. Another was the Vidinge mansion, the roof of which you could just barely see. Up on a slight elevation on Kalv Island, you could see Per-Anders' cottage, Rickard's home these days.

The history of the area was the creation of men. There were evidences of forest fires; there were tales of family feuds, of marauders, of assaults and drownings that had happened only a few years or months ago. Other tales dealt with matters somewhat less tangible: the mysterious aura of light above the ridges, which seemed to be an omen of misfortune; the eeriness of the forest; the wood nymph and the fairies, not to mention all the small trolls residing beneath the roots and in the crevices.

Jon and Rickard, enjoying their first real summer vacation, were completely unconcerned with history or stories. They were comfortably clad in knickers; they wore no socks. There was sand in their hair and between their toes, and there were dried fish scales in the creases of their shirts —garments that Jon seldom and Rickard almost never changed. At the moment they were rowing the doctor's white and green painted skiff, heading toward Sand Cape.

"I'm sure," Jon said, "that there must have been summer vacations before, but I guess we were too young to understand the idea."

Rickard craned his neck to one side, implying that he agreed. "In principle." He had just lately learned the ex‚ pression and had discovered it to be particularly useful, even if he weren't absolutely sure what it meant. "Yes, in principle. I guess I had a summer vacation last year, too."

Jon gave his silent assent. Naturally each had different experiences to reflect upon when it came to summer vacations. Rickard had never been in the country before the day, almost two years previously, when he had first come to live with Per-Anders. Before this he had lived—if you could call it living—in a tenement on Quarry Road in Soltuna. His summer vacations had been periods that seemed never to end: times spent in alleys, in back yards and vacant lots, where nothing grew—nothing, in any case, that was soft and green and fragrant.

"Why *is* it, anyway, that nothing grows in the city limits of Soltuna?" Jon asked, letting his thoughts on the subject of summer vacations wander at will. "It isn't built up everywhere, and there are a good many vacant lots and the like. You'd think that seed could be carried from the country by the wind."

"Thistles and burrs," Rickard said abruptly. "Solid rock foundation. Too hard for them to take root. Still there are wild raspberries in a couple of places. But they aren't anywhere near as big as the ones that grow along the swamps, of course."

Jon's thoughts were still roving, but he did not express them aloud. He wondered about Rickard's family, his mother and his brothers and sisters. Several of them were younger, a couple older. Didn't he miss them at all? Oh, his younger brothers and sisters, you could understand about them, but his mother? After all, she *was* his very own mother! He never spoke of her. Never did he say, "My mother always . . ." or, "I told my mother that . . ."

But Jon was aware that he visited his old home once a week, regularly, during the school year. On those occasions he always had with him a basket of eggs or fruit or a bouquet of wildflowers when he came to the village in the farmer's wagon. There was a tacit agreement between them that on those days each would go his own way after the last class period. Otherwise, they were generally together, taking a walk around the square or sometimes walking straight home to the doctor's house, where Rickard waited until time for him to ride home in the carriage. He had a fantastic route to school, Rickard did! Every day, when possible, he rowed between Kalv Island and the mainland, and in the winter he walked across the ice. That he never mentioned his oldest brother—the one fre-

quently sought by the police for robberies and assaults,
who had now disappeared from the Soltuna area with
wife and children—was perfectly understandable. His
other brothers were often in trouble, too. But his mother!
Jon, whose existence was inextricably tied to his own
mother, wondered about it. But one thing about Rickard
—any vocal expression came long, long after his actions,
let alone his thoughts. When he had a vague, distant expression in his eyes, when the wrinkles at the base of his
nose became square and deep, Jon imagined that his
friend's thoughts were back on Quarry Road, in the single
room with the six mattresses. And if Rickard had not made
his home with Per-Anders, following the dramatic evening when Father removed the old man's appendix, with
the assistance of Jon and Rickard, there would have been
seven mattresses in the room. This Jon knew for sure.
Rickard had told him that much, but not a great deal
more.

One time the boys had gone together and bought a
drawing pad and pencil as a birthday present for one of
Rickard's younger brothers. There would have been no
present if Jon hadn't chipped in twenty-five öre. Rickard
hadn't invited Jon home with him to deliver the gift, but
a week later, with a curt "from my brother," he had
passed three drawings over to Jon's desk. All of them were
of horses and cowboys. The horses reared, they galloped,
they stood still and grazed.

"But those are terribly good," Jon said. "Is he honestly
only eight years old? This horse is really full of life! I'll
save them. Thank him for me, will you?"

Blushing, Rickard nodded his head. Although beaming with obvious pride, he said nothing more.

Jon and Rickard tied the boat up at the wash barge. As Rickard threw the fore rope around one of the poles, Jon took the boat hook and fished up the chain from the buoy bobbing around in the water. He fastened the catch on the ring in the thwart. Reeds grew all the way out to the buoy. Jon grabbed a reed with an enormous blade head and hacked it off with his penknife.

For a while he and Rickard stayed in the skiff, amusing themselves by making reeds into little boats and setting them afloat as they leaned over the side. Some of them capsized immediately, while others glided along surely and proudly out toward the open water. Rickard would grab the reeds right near the root shaft. Jon was clumsier, and at times his hands shook. His boats were somewhat lopsided, but by way of compensation he set them afloat on the surface of the water with the utmost caution. The result was about even for both.

"Three of yours on the way to sea, three of mine," Jon said. The waves slapped gently at the side of the boat. From the greenish darkness along the shore came a cool draft.

"Your first one is going to take the lead when it rounds the barge," Rickard declared.

They had played this game dozens of times, and at this point it was just about to die of inertia, especially with the sun high in the sky and the midday heat beginning to be oppressive.

"Hey, let's go up. What do you say?"

Inside the washhouse, Mari and a crofter's wife from Vidinge were laughing merrily and loudly. They were just about to put a huge wash to soak. At the corner of the building, yellow and white elderberry bushes bloomed, and along the way toward the doctor's red cottage, the ditchbanks sparkled brightly with cumin and wild chervil. The grass had not yet been mowed a second time because the help the doctor's family usually hired was still completely occupied on the farms and other properties. The bumblebees, grateful for the respite, were enjoying themselves to the full. A buzzing chorus arose from the beds of saxifrage, pinks, from the pink and white clover, from the yellow mustard, from the violet blooms of the vetch.

Jon and Rickard, contented and happy, lazily directed their steps up to their own place of refuge, which they had found beneath the veranda facing the water. It had an earthen floor and dark corners filled with spiderwebs. In the winter the space was used for storing summer furniture. A few broken items were still there.

With a saw the boys had turned an old broken-backed, wooden sofa into two low-legged chairs. A barrel with the cooper's bands still on it that had once contained salt herring served as a table.

The lighting beneath the veranda was inadequate, a fact that caused the boys serious concern since they used their little hideaway mainly for reading. A number of books, not appropriate for displaying to the outside world, lay in a discarded clothesbasket.

It was cool and lovely there beneath the veranda floor. The summer heat couldn't overcome the dampness arising from the firmly packed earthen floor or the cool draft from the cellar, which lay behind. On the barrel stood a dusty bottle of currant juice, brought in directly from the same cellar. In one of the remote corners, they had managed, by pooling their strength, to loosen four stone slabs. Through the hole, barely a foot wide, Jon, with his narrow shoulders, was able to crawl into Mari's larder of butter tubs, crocks of cream, barrels of herring, smoked ham, preserves, and juices.

They had an unspoken agreement that the raids on the cellar would always be made by Jon alone. No one in the household could deny him access to the delicacies. Rickard, on the other hand, was viewed with doubtful, to say nothing of suspicious, glances by the servants in the doctor's house.

Even Mari, who had the greatest respect for the judgment of the members of the family, would occasionally shake her head. Never did she do this when the doctor's receptionist-nurse could see her, because the nurse was a very snobbish person—no two ways about it. But she would pour out her heart to the faithful stableboy, Soren.

"The doctor has a heart of gold, but it wouldn't hurt my feelings if he were to use a little more common sense now and then. I think that Rickard looks a little sneaky. Maybe he's all right in certain respects, but he's not proper company for our innocent Jon, let me tell you. And that father! He's a real boozer if I ever saw one!

"And then there's his brother! He hasn't been seen in the area now for quite a while, and I'm sure he's in hiding somewhere. However, I did hear that someone spotted him at one of labor leader Palm's gatherings out on the commons. Riot and rebellion, I call it. One of these days we'll all be murdered in our beds! But the doctor sticks up for this Rickard, and perhaps even Palm for all I know, so I guess it's best to keep your mouth shut!"

Rickard and Jon were not given to defiance. Therefore, it was always Jon who went after provisions in the cellar and the larder and who appropriated the necessary items from the garden plots.

Picking up a pot-bellied copper can with a lid and a bent spout, he shook it.

"Empty. Almost. I'll have to get a little water up in the kitchen. Soren brought the water barrel this morning, I noticed. And I'll pick a few strawberries at the same time. I saw a few left under the rhubarb leaves. They ripen later there."

"In the meantime, I'll clean up in here," Rickard said as he looked around in the half darkness. From one of the wooden shelves, he took down a kerosene lamp. "This needs to be dusted off—and filled."

A great mark of confidence had been shown the boys when they were allowed to have a lamp in their hideaway. Mother had protested—she was terrified of fire and smoke. But Father was concerned about the boys' eyesight, and he had also realized that a shaded, mysterious den in this efficiently run household, rural though it was, might be a good thing for Jon, but even more for Rickard.

The boys repaid the confidence by caring for the kerosene lamp as though it were an infant.

Rickard wiped it off, polished the shade, and filled the

kerosene well without spilling a drop of the dangerous substance. Before lighting the lamp, he placed it on the barrel. Then he adjusted the flame.

The soft yellow light was a relief after the intense sunlight outside. The glow fell on Detective Gordon's *Assassination in the Chapel,* Jon's reading matter for the moment, and on Rickard's *Emperor Napoleon's Sceptre.* In the clothesbasket, which had been pulled over close to the "table," was a pile of Nick Carter books. These were considered genuine treasures, since there was talk that the authorities might brand them as forbidden reading for young people.

Jon walked around the veranda stairs. Yan, Jon's young brother, was enjoying his afternoon nap beneath the linden trees, lulled to sleep by the buzz of insects in the treetops and protected from the elements by a net covering. The pastel-colored sweet peas emitted clouds of fragrance.

From the arbor Mother's voice could be heard. Jon slowed his steps.

There was something in her tone of voice that wakened him from his summer reveries.

The high, bloom-covered grass was waving in the breeze. Beneath the trees at the corner of the house, the linden blossoms with their heavy, winglike leaves had begun to pile up. Jon had a foreboding that something was about to change.

2

An Unusual Errand

I T wasn't that Mother was speaking more loudly than usual. It was the tone of her voice that made Jon take notice. He understood the nuances of her speech so well.

Mother said, "I wish very much that you had time to ride down there and see for yourself what's going on."

"But that's impossible," Father replied. "I have to go out on my sick calls. The farmers have saved up their ailments this past week rather than make the journey into Soltuna. I'm sure when I get to Vidinge, there won't be just old Mrs. Ivarson and her swollen leg to look after. There'll be a long line of people with various problems wanting advice and some ointment."

"I realize. But, Olof, there are things that are irrevocable. If Alfrida just *can't* afford to pay for the boy, as Mari insisted . . ."

"Mother dear," Father's voice said—with a tinge of laughter in it—"you imagine all sorts of things just because you're so concerned with the poor and needy. The times are gone—fortunately—when they could be sold."

Once again Jon heard Mother's voice through the shiny leaves. And there was the disquieting tone once more. It was unlike Mother not to play along with the things Father said in jest or in an attempt to gloss over something. But she sounded, instead, harsh and keyed up.

"I wouldn't be too sure if I were you. I'm not fond of that new chairman of the District Council. One thing only is on his mind—money—and he pays no attention to the new dean. But you—he has respect for you. For the things you straighten out, that's easy to see! You have science behind you. That's why you have some responsibility, Olof! In the name of God!"

By this time Jon scarcely dared to breathe. His lower jaw had dropped, and he was staring just as he did when he was a little child and something had bewildered him.

Every evening Mother said aloud, "God, we thank thee," for Yan, although he understood almost nothing and generally fell asleep in the middle of "Praise to thee forever more." Almost every Sunday she attended services in the Soltuna church, when Jon, if he wanted to, was allowed to accompany her. But hearing her mention the name of God like this—and to Father, at that—and in this tone of voice!

Breathless, Jon continued to stare.

Silence reigned in the arbor. Linden blossoms floated through the air. The peep-peep of the nestling swallows came from the tiles on the roof of the veranda.

"If anything that heathen were in the works, Liljenstam would have warned me. But he said nothing. In any case, I would have gone down to the district meeting for your sake if I thought there were the remotest possibility of what you say. But after I'm through at Vidinge, I have to go another three miles to Hedsel—a strangulated hernia —this evening."

Mother must have turned away, for her last words sounded remote.

"Well, I guess there's nothing to do, dear. We'll just have to hope for the best. Be careful, now! I'm sure Soren has everything in order. Just a little while ago I saw him hitch up Figaro . . ."

Jon sensed that they kissed each other.

Father emerged from the arbor with hasty and purposeful steps. He was bent forward, with his short black beard pointed down toward the ground. He saw Jon, at which point his face lighted up as if Jon had reminded him of something. However, he said nothing. In too much of a hurry, he merely gave a wave of his hand.

Jon knew that his brown medical bag was ready and waiting for him on the front steps facing the woods. He could hear Figaro snorting.

It was too bad about Father. At this time, during the few weeks of warm summer, he should have been on vacation. A young doctor with an excellent reputation had moved in to occupy a couple of rooms in their home in Soltuna, and he was to take care of Father's practice from there.

But about that time, an unfortunate thing happened. Dr. Liljenstam, the provincial doctor in Vidinge and Hedsel, fell ill—an old heart condition flared up again— and landed in the Soltuna hospital. Father, who had just

begun his vacation, had to pitch in and help. A week without a doctor had already brought the district to the edge of catastrophe. Until the medical commission could find a substitute, Father, who chanced to be at Sand Cape, had to uphold the medical tradition and serve as provincial doctor.

Early, early in the mornings, while the choruses of birds were singing their hymn of praise to the heavens, Jon, who slept in a garret room facing the woods, would hear Father's and Soren's muffled voices through the open window and the rustle of the gravel beneath the wheels of the gig. At times he could even smell the pungent odor of the horse, still warm from the stable. His senses would begin to awaken happily from his friendly, faraway dreamland to the edge of consciousness, to just one thought: "I'm not going to wake up yet for a long, long time."

Now, on this sun-drenched day, Jon watched Figaro and the gig disappear between the lindens down the road. He went to see his mother in the arbor.

She stood with her back to him, slender in her thin white blouse and blue-and-white striped cotton skirt that reached all the way to the ground. She was gathering up cups and saucers after their coffee.

"Mother," Jon said. "What was it that you and Father were talking about?"

The clatter of dishes ceased. Mother brushed the crumbs from the tablecloth. She spoke after a second's hesitation.

"Nothing. Nothing special."

Jon walked around the wooden table. He didn't like to force himself into their confidence, but neither did he care to be put off.

"I know," he said. "It was something you were worried about. I heard."

Mother piled the dishes and the bread basket onto a tray. She still seemed hesitant.

"Well, it isn't exactly easy to explain, you see, Jon. It has to do with the district and public assistance and the like."

"Yes, but you could at least try to explain, couldn't you?"

Mother sighed. She was tired, worried about her overworked husband, and disturbed. But her patience was unfailing.

"Look here, Jon. You know who Alfrida is, don't you?"

"The old lady from Ulvahult?"

"Yes. For about six years now, she has been taking care of a little boy whose mother died of tuberculosis when he was born, and she has had him in her home all that time. She has been just like—well, just like a mother to him all these years, although you know what miserable conditions the crofters live under. But, anyway, she has kept a pig, and she makes lace and sells lace edging, and even lace collars, too. You know about it."

Jon nodded. That was the only reason he knew Alfrida. Mother bought bundles of lace, both for borders and finer edgings, from her every autumn. All of Mother's sheets were adorned with this ivory-white handmade lace.

"I honestly don't know how I can explain all this to you." Mother noticed the serious expression in Jon's eyes. "It sounds even crazier when you try to put it into words. But the boy—Alfrida's boy—is not actually hers. He is the ward of the district."

Mother smoothed the tablecloth fringe. As she continued, she seeemd to comb it with her fingers.

"The district has to provide for orphaned children . . ."

"Yes, but the district hasn't had to all the while that—that Alfrida has had him, right? Those stingy old men in the District Council! Father says that about them all the time."

Mother smiled.

"And he's probably right. It has been very convenient, especially for the district, to have escaped responsibility for the poor boy all these years. But now, you see, they feel that he should begin to make his own way. They want to . . ." Mother's voice sank. "They want payment for him."

Jon's lower jaw fell.

"Payment?"

"Yes. They feel that he can be of use, and they want the person who now has him to pay for him."

Mother had sat down. She combed and smoothed the fringe. Jon stood observing her white fingers. Once more he heard the tone of voice that had upset him outside the arbor so much that it seemed as if sounds and lights and smells had all been changed at once.

As his mother had, he lowered his voice as though he were speaking of something indecent.

"Do you mean that the district wants to collect a payment from Alfrida?

"Yes, that's the way it is. Or, to be more accurate, I'm *afraid* that's the way things are going to go. Mari came to me with the story yesterday. She had met Alfrida up at the Dunders' yard. There was a man from another province there selling his wares, and a number of women had assembled in the kitchen."

"But, Mother, you said that the boy was only six years old, didn't you?"

"Six and a half."

"Well, he can't be put to work, can he? What could he do to earn money?"

"He can be a herder boy."

Jon nodded. He knew a good bit about the herders, although their lives were as different as could be imagined from his own as a schoolboy in Soltuna. Perhaps that was why he knew about them. Rickard was acquainted with a couple of herders from the croft below Uddesund and had told about them in detail. Jon had also seen them at a distance when he had been out in the big woods picking wild strawberries. Above all, he had heard them. The cattle usually made a terrible amount of noise. They knocked among the branches; they thundered along the ground; they bellowed and bleated as they wandered about, and the herders were not given to silence either. They talked, laughed, and sang; they blew their cattle horns and their birchbark trumpets—which was a rather unusual art—and cracked long whips. Every morning they took the cattle from the Vidinge estate and from the farms and properties in the area up to the big woods that opened onto the grazing lands in the valleys, through groves and woods, through marshes and meadowlands.

The herders were often farmers' children about ten years of age, but where there were none, the farmers would hire boys and girls from the crofts. For the most part, they were younger. Their duties were to lead the oxen or the cows or sheep to pasture at dawn, to see that they didn't destroy property in the woods, knock down stone fences, or wander too far, and then to drive the animals home again at dusk. The herders, both boys and girls, wore wide-brimmed straw hats; they carried food bags tightly clenched in their fists and wore sundials around their necks. The sundials, of course, were for telling time.

These children had a heavy responsibility because the cattle were valuable. They carried it out by clinging together, ten, perhaps twenty of them, each with his own herd.

Rickard had thought about serving as a herder at Vidinge, but it would have meant being away from Per-Anders every single day all summer, so nothing came of it.

But a six-year-old!

Jon said, "I thought Father mentioned the district meeting, didn't he? Is that where Alfrida's boy is going to be?"

"The Public Assistance Commission is going to have a meeting there this afternoon to decide what is going to happen to those poor souls—both children and adults—who are unable to support themselves and who have no relatives."

"But the little boy has Alfrida, doesn't he?"

"Yes, but she just took him out of the goodness of her heart. 'Just,' you understand, Jon!" Mother sounded bitter. "Father says that there's no doubt the boy ought to remain with her and that the district ought to be grateful to her for it. He claims that the time of auctions is past!"

"Auctions?"

"Yes, it's where people announce the things they have for sale, with the one entering the highest bid—that is, willing to pay the most—getting the article he bids on. . . . Just imagine—they'll call out that Alfrida's boy is for sale, just as if he were a bureau or a table, and the one who will get him is the one willing to pay the most toward his keep and to charge the district the least."

Mother was still speaking softly, but every word carried great seriousness. "And you understand, don't you, Jon, that anyone who is heartless enough to bid money for a little boy is doing it with profit in mind—with the idea of putting him to work and earning money from him!"

Here Mother shook the tablecloth fringe.

"If there had been a chance, I would have gone down to the district headquarters myself! But it's three miles from here, and I truly don't know what I would do if I were there. If only Father . . ."

Jon glanced at his mother's fragile, light figure, at her enormous crown of ash-blond hair, which made her head altogether too heavy for her narrow neck.

No, that would have been utterly insane! It would never do for Mother to go down to the district headquarters and rub shoulders with the snuff-chewing, booted old men of the district. It would have been as ridiculous as if she had dressed up in a long priest's habit and climbed up into the pulpit.

"Well," said Jon, "I can go down and see what's going on. Rickard and I. It might just be interesting. However, I don't really think it's necessary. I'm sure Father is right. We aren't living in the eighteenth century," he added knowingly.

In his heart of hearts, Jon agreed with Father. It was so easy for Mother to imagine all sorts of things, and besides she didn't realize the progress that had been made in the world. Mari was always jarring her with her stories, most of which had taken place years back. And Alfrida was the sort who worried and complained about every-thing imaginable.

Naturally, though, it was best to find out what was hap-pening so as to set Mother's mind at rest.

"You'll have to hurry, Jon!" Mother said. "And listen now. . . ." Mother glanced critically at Jon's berry-stained pants and soiled shirt. "Put on some clean clothes. Lend Rickard something to put on so that you won't look too horrible. Otherwise, they might try to stop you from en-tering the District Council headquarters.

"And hurry, Jon. Please, please hurry!"

3

Jon and Rickard

Less than ten minutes later, Jon and Rickard were running down the same road where Father, Figaro, and the gig had recently disappeared. Jon was wearing his new summer trousers. They reached a bit below his knees. Rickard had on one of Soren's cast-off homespun jackets. It was hardly elegant, but it didn't look as if he had outgrown it as anything Jon had to offer him would have. Rickard was taller and more broad-shouldered than Jon.

Outgrown clothing was regarded as the worst thing in the world. Anything else—worn, dirty, even torn—was better than outgrown garments. This was a sign of poverty, and a condition that both city and country people ridiculed and laughed at. Mother and Mari always made Jon's new clothing a size or two too large to allow for shrinkage, and it made Jon feel important to be able to say that they were "to grow into."

Jon and Rickard were perspiring. It was uncomfortable

to rush along a country road in the worst of the midday heat dressed in these clothes.

They had on their silk-crowned school caps with the school insignia. The white metal initials, SCLS, seemed very elegant indeed as the one letter twined into the next.

Jon had happened to think of the caps at the last second. Fortunately, Rickard had left his at Sand Cape on the last day of school, where it had remained ever since.

Jon mused that the caps might come in handy as a sort of entrance pass to the District Council grounds.

A short while later, both boys removed the caps from their heads and stuck them under their arms. Here near the coast and in the big woods, the insignia of the school meant absolutely nothing.

The first mention Jon made of the journey's purpose

was after they had walked a good distance and had slackened their speed. Previously, he had merely stated that they were to do an errand for Mother in the village.

Rickard listened attentively. He didn't once interrupt the account nor, to Jon's great surprise, did he bat an eye over Mother's anxiety and suspicion.

Jon had noticed this tendency in Rickard before. He seldom saw any promise in the prospects for the poor and was, in fact, inclined to fear the worst. No one, certainly none of his classmates at the Misses Martells' Private School, had been so astonished as Rickard himself when he easily passed the entrance examination to the Latin School and was given a scholarship that guaranteed his schooling there.

"Well, as far as I'm concerned," said Jon, "I think that Mari frightened Mother with her stories and that the whole thing is exaggerated."

Rickard let out one of his deep sighs. Since he was a little out of breath, it sounded like a snore.

"Nobody knows for sure what can happen down at the Public Assistance Commission."

"What I don't understand," Jon said thoughtfully, "is why the boy Alfrida has taken care of wasn't sent to the poorhouse instead. That's a stroke of luck for him, actually, because he almost certainly is better off with Alfrida, but in Soltuna, homeless children are sent to the poorhouse—or to the new children's home nowadays.

"I know . . ." Jon added, "because Father often goes on sick calls at the poorhouse, and I. . . ." He halted, finishing a little lamely, "I have been with him in there several times."

He had been on the brink of saying, "I have been there giving out toys and pants and skirts for Christmas."

It occurred to him that these presents, which Mother used to sew and collect through a women's organization, were also given out in the homes of the poor along Quarry Road, where Rickard's old home was.

Rickard didn't notice the subject around which Jon had skillfully maneuvered. He knew much more about poverty than Jon and was about to share some of his knowledge with him.

"There's no poorhouse in this district!"

"What? What do you mean?"

"Just what I said. They're too stingy. It's cheaper for them to board out the people who can't take care of themselves—send them out to the farms and the cottages. The district gives a minimal subsidy to those who take in the poor—as little as possible, you see. And that's why they hold auctions. The one who enters the lowest bid for the maintenance subsidy and makes it cheapest for the district gets the dependent. Usually the district doles out between five and ten crowns a month, and that's cheaper for them than building poorhouses.

Jon remained silent. He didn't know much about the conditions out here in the country.

Rickard continued. "Once a year the Public Assistance Commission holds an auction. The poor and needy are offered again for one year. Quite often they have to move, of course. They call that 'county rotation.' The district is divided into counties, and the poor people have to move from place to place at the convenience of the district."

By now the boys were moving along at quite a fast clip.

"Where did you ever learn all this?" Jon asked, astonished—but not for the first time—at Rickard's power to assemble details, catalog them lucidly, and remember them unerringly.

"Per-Anders has told me some things, and others I heard Mr. Palm talk about on the commons in Soltuna. He is pretty elderly now, but other speakers have followed his tactics, too."

Jon's lower jaw dropped.

"Have you gone to those meetings?"

"Yes, and at the Community House, too. I want to know all about things. And there you learn things—things they never talk about in school."

"But listen, Rickard, it's socialist workers who sponsor these meetings. There have been riots a couple of times. The newspapers refer to it as rebellion. The police were called . . ."

Following the road along the coast, they had arrived at the gate in the fence surrounding Sand Cape. There was an inner enclosure, too, but that gate had been opened. Between the enclosures was Figaro's pasture. It was so large, with its woods, glades, and meadows, that Soren put a cowbell on Figaro so as to be able to find him when he was needed. Figaro . . . he, too, should have been on vacation this lovely summer day.

Between the thickets of alder and hazels along the road, they could see the glistening waters of the lake, stretching in ribbons—some silvery, some coal black.

Jon gave it all a parting glance.

"Today we should have gone swimming before the afternoon," he thought.

Beyond the Sand Cape property, the road, hard and dusty, swung up toward the big woods. Along the ditchbanks there were groves of pines, straight as rods, with their dark tops stretched toward the endless blue July sky.

But Jon's attention was completely concentrated on what Rickard had told him.

It must have been on the evenings when he stayed overnight in his old home on Quarry Road that he attended the notorious meetings—evenings when Jon had sat reading on the sofa in the sitting room at home, with a fire roaring in the ceramic stove. When he looked up from his book, he saw two round eyes of fire, the only openings in the coal-black door. . . .

What had Rickard seen out on the breezy commons in the square outside the Community House?

These thoughts disturbed Jon. He tried to imagine any of his other freshman classmates at the school going to a meeting of labor agitators. The druggist's son Edvard—the manufacturer's son Magnus—the elementary school teacher's son Nils—

None of them was a mama's boy or a clod, but naturally they never had permission to be out wandering the streets whenever they pleased.

Jon found it impossible to drop the subject.

"What do they talk about at those meetings?"

"Oh, all sorts of things having to do with how people get along and how conditions ought to be. About unemployment mostly, about public assistance. One time I heard about these auctions. For that matter, it was a . . . a woman who spoke that time."

"A *woman!* On the commons?"

"No, that was in the Community House. She had just been investigating how orphaned children are cared for. She said that this business of auctions was . . . was inhuman and completely heartless."

"That's exactly what Mother said."

Just imagine! Mother and the woman who spoke at the Community House thought alike!

Jon tried to envision what the woman could have looked like. He pictured her wearing men's clothing. In any case, a starched collar and jacket.

"What else do they talk about?" Jon was not ready to give up.

"Mostly about unemployment, about wages, and about strikes. They say we must strike—stop working—until we get better wages."

Jon glanced at Rickard from the side. He had said "we."

Jon knew a good deal about the strike—the big strike that had taken place. He just had to tell what he had heard.

"Father says that the Swedish people are too poor and that they can't afford to strike. He says that changes have to come from the inside first—inside the people them-selves. Lots of workers drink up all the wages they get. He has seen a lot, you know. He maintains that strikes will only lead to misery and famine, that the workers have to take it easy, even though they are right about many things . . ."

"We've taken it easy for long enough."

The boys walked rapidly in step, each in his own wagon-wheel rut. It was cooler in the big woods where the moss retained the dampness and where only isolated sunbeams, quivery and weak, penetrated the foliage. Along here at the beginning of summer, Rickard and Jon had found five different kinds of wintergreen for their herbarium.

"The very thing we're talking about now—that the dis-tricts should be paid for a child of six years just because he can be put to sweat and slave! Can you just go on and *wait* for such conditions to disappear?"

Rickard turned his head and looked at his friend with an expression that Jon couldn't exactly puzzle out. And the expression, "sweat and slave!" This was not used in the Latin School or among educated people.

Jon said, somewhat hastily, "Father said that the days of the auctions are over! Nowadays everyone wants people to live under respectable conditions. They don't want anyone to starve or freeze, and they don't want children to be forced to work instead of attending school."

Rickard shrugged his shoulders. "We'll see for our-selves," he said, "when we get to the District Council head-quarters. Look, Jon." He made a sweeping motion with his hand toward a deep cliff where moss-covered boulders rose behind a wind-fallen pine. "Doesn't that make you think of this?"

" 'Let the free woods help to make us freer
From Life's conflict and its pedantry!
Let's pretend that through these glades we wander,
Wild red Indians, be it understood,
And our wigwam is the cavern yonder—
I the Big-Wig, Sachem of the Wood . . .'

"That's the way it looks right there, don't you think?"

Reluctantly, Jon gave a slight nod. The poet Fröding. Rickard and his memory!

He was really like no other boy Jon knew. Never would Edvard or Magnus or Nils recite several lines of Fröding; even if they could, they wouldn't dare. They would feel too embarrassed.

Mari referred to Rickard as "Svensson's boy," usually with a little snort. Jon realized that in actual fact he was no one's boy—not his mother's, not his father's, not even Per-Anders', though he was obviously deeply attached to the old man on Kalv Island. He was his own master.

Jon admired him for this. No longer did he himself like being called "doctor's boy." Father was wise and wonderful—no two ways about it—but at times Jon felt a little resentful at Father's being mentioned in every possible connection. In Jon's inner thoughts, his father didn't loom quite so large as one might imagine. As a matter of fact, Jon was smitten with the word "I." "I" sounded bold, vigorous, purposeful. In composition class at school,

Jon chose subjects that gave him the opportunity to write, "I think . . . I usually . . ."

Jon realized that Rickard had ingeniously changed the subject by reciting Fröding's verse. He was probably trying to say, "Let's not quarrel, Jon! These are things you just can't understand properly. You can't help it, but that's the way it is. Let's enjoy what we have in common—the woods, the summer, the vacation, and the things we've learned at school."

Jon still wasn't contented.

Silently and a bit more rapidly, they walked along the treeless slopes leading down to the village of Vidinge. They had felt confident in the dark woods. Now on level ground, Jon felt anxiety and uncertainty beginning to creep up on him.

It was almost three o'clock. Men, dripping with sweat, walked the fields reaping. After them came the women. They raked up the grain that had fallen into yellow-gold piles. The rows of men and women moved forward rhythmically in a semicircle. The women, daughters, and servants from the farms and neighboring properties and crofters' wives from the forest had their skirts tied up and wore shawls on their heads. The heat of the sun beat down. The piled-up clouds along the horizon seemed unchangeable and immovable.

The boys came to the big road leading into the village. In fields between the farms, near the stone walls with yellow and pink houseleek blooming in the cracks, sheep and cows stood in bunches. A couple of horse-drawn wagons passed the boys before they arrived at the first cottage

that was part of the village. Behind the wagons the dust
rose in a white cloud above the ditches, where camomile,
thistles, and milkweed had long since been obscured by a
gray veil.

"Those people," said Rickard with a nod in the direction of the vehicle. "I'll just bet they are on their way to
the district meeting. I recognized both the farmer from
Uddesund and that fat old Jansson from Heda. He is the
chairman of both the District Council and the Public Assistance Commission. He's rich and he's mean. Per-Anders
doesn't like him at all, but he maintains that Jansson
won't give up before he's a City Councilman and a Member of Parliament."

"But if people don't like him . . . ? Doesn't someone that wants to be a Member of Parliament have to be a nice person?"

Rickard gave the usual shrug of his shoulders.

"Like him, like him not. . . . Don't you realize that the most important thing for a man like that is that he be stingy? That way he gains the approval of the others—farmers, tradesmen, and the richest of the craftsmen. They're the ones who have to bear the burden of the expenses for the poor of the district. Jon, look! They've already begun the meeting. What if we get there too late?"

They could see the District Council grounds from the top of a hill, but to get to the gate, they had to follow the road leading around the dingy yellow schoolhouse on its triangular lot. The latest vehicles to arrive were parked outside the fence. The sand plot inside was already choked with wagons and carriages and carts. You could recognize the miller's wagon, which, as usual, was covered with white dust, the carpenter's surrey with its dapple gray filly, and a couple of simple carts belonging to the woodsmen.

A man's black bicycle leaned against the ancient maple at the corner of the building. Both of the boys had noticed it. It was not a common sight in this farming village, but in some vague way it seemed familiar to them.

Jon looked around in vain for the Vidinge patron's old four-wheeler with its coat-of-arms on the doors. It would have been comforting to see it standing there because the patron was a friend of Father's and a nobleman. But—Jon recalled on second thought—the patron was on a trip abroad.

He felt a disturbing sensation at the pit of his stomach as he put on his school cap. Rickard followed suit.

Some of the village boys were trying to sneak through the holes in the fence surrounding the schoolyard, which was a favorite hideaway, even during summer vacation. The schoolteacher, who lived with his family in an apartment in one wing, was beloved by the children and kept in touch with his pupils all year around.

But even the boldest of the half-grown boys didn't dare to try entering the district headquarters.

It would be a mistake to say that it looked even the least bit inviting—a range of brown buildings on a stone foundation, with a row of bare, curtainless windows. On the sand plot among the vehicles stood several women conversing in muffled tones. Their whole bearing, including the glances they directed toward the headquarters' high doors, betrayed an anxious respect. They grew silent at the sight of the two boys.

Jon and Rickard were embarrassed. Looking neither to the left nor to the right, they walked straight up to the entrance.

4

Tomorrow Is Too Late

I T was a few minutes before Jon had the courage to look around once he and Rickard had managed to push their way through the crowd of observers and into the District Council headquarters. Had matters depended upon Jon, they would never have gotten any farther than just inside the door. But Rickard, who was used to meetings, managed to get near the lower end of the long black table without hurrying and without calling unnecessary attention to themselves. From there, once they were settled, the boys could evaluate the situation.

The District Council members were the only people in the room seated. All the others were standing. The observers were in an anxious, bashful clump inside the door, which was propped open because of the summer heat. At the other end of the room, there was also an assembly of people, and Jon could see there were two distinct groups. From what Rickard had told him, he realized that one of the groups was that of the "dependents." There was no mistaking the fact, dressed as they were in ragged clothing and exhibiting none of the curiosity so obvious in the observers at the door. Most of them looked ancient. Several women seemed to be nothing but skin and bones, and some old men had untrimmed beards, canes, and trembling hands. Little by little, Jon discovered that a couple of the elderly persons were deformed. One of them was supported by some makeshift crutches, and one old lady was obviously, as Mari always said, a little "weak in the head," because she giggled audibly and hummed to herself.

Whatever Jon had expected or hoped to see, this was not it. These toothless mouths, these deformed backs were conditions he had never seen except when, as "the doctor's boy," he had visited the poorhouse in Soltuna. And there, he had always had in the background the comforting certainty: "They are being taken care of. Father himself looks after them once each week."

Here he felt as if he had lost his foothold. The only consolation was that, no matter where he looked, Jon couldn't see any children in the assembly.

The other group over there was of a totally different character. They were woodsmen, homeowners, grain dealers, and merchants. The miller was there, as was the smith. Jon recognized him because he had accompanied Soren and Figaro to the smithy when Figaro had his spikenails removed for the summer.

A heavy smell lingered in the room. Oiled leather, tobacco, clothes that had not been aired out, musty wooden houses, and perspiration had created a peculiar combina-

tion. In comparison to the sweet-scented summer day outside, it was stupefying. Involuntarily, Jon looked at Rickard. There was something healthy and reassuring in the
sight of his thin profile, the profile Jon was so used to
seeing at his side almost every day.

Was Rickard, "Svensson's boy," experiencing the same
emotions and need for comfort as the "doctor's boy"? Yes.
His eyes sought the curve of Jon's dark, round head, the
unexpectedly strong, straight lines of his neck. It wasn't
the first time Rickard had gained reassurance and confidence by looking at that neck.

How would it all end? Rickard was more upset than
Jon because he was standing a little to one side, and he
had seen something Jon had not yet discovered. From the
window ledge at the far side of the room dangled a couple
of childish legs in thick gray socks. Rickard craned his
neck as hard as he could but to no avail. The owner of
the legs was not visible.

Fat Mr. Jansson from Heda, the district chairman, sat
at the head of the table in a high-backed chair with red
cushions, while the county representatives sat on un-
painted three-legged pine stools. Jon counted seventeen
of them, not including the chairman. Each was wearing
his heavy, dark Sunday suit. Several of them were strong,
powerful, huge-framed men, and the rickety stools on
spindly legs seemed to groan under the weight of their
broad backs. The men were obviously along in years. The
trust of the district was not something one merited in
one's youth. They wore felt hats or long peaked caps on
their heads; most of them had grizzled gray whiskers or

beards, though a few sported chin whiskers and sideburns.

The sight of this awe-inspiring group gave Jon and Rickard pause, and it was a good while before they regained enough confidence to be able to listen to the proceedings.

One of the district officials who sat on one side of the long table was speaking gruffly into his red beard. He was telling of a person called Lars from Fishing Croft. The fishing business had gone disastrously for Lars. His "old lady" —the information emerged from the beard, accompanied by much clearing of his throat and a certain snorting sound from his nose, all of which made it obvious that the speaker felt superior to the man whose plight he was describing—his "old lady" and the children had no means of support.

"And for that matter, if Lars does earn anything, he drinks it up!" The bearded man sighed. "I request that the council give Lars from Fishing Croft ten crowns a month out of public assistance funds!"

Jansson from Heda now spoke in a resounding, bass voice. "What say the members?"

"Much too steep!" said someone from the foot of the table amid spirited comments from right and left. "Six crowns is a great plenty!"

"Six crowns a month for a family of seven persons isn't adequate, it just isn't adequate. They can't live on that in these expensive times."

The chairman's voice boomed out once more. "The man is obliged to contribute to the support of his family. The taxpayers of the district can't assume the burden when the man of the family is able to work."

One solitary voice was raised in defense of the family from Fishing Croft. "What good does it do to say that Lars is considered able to work. We're aware, all of us, that the little he does earn goes for alcohol. What about the wife and children . . ."

Jon poked Rickard, who nodded slowly. They had both recognized the voice of the farmer from Uddesund.

But it was clearly a voice crying in the wilderness. The farmer received absolutely no support. Jansson from Heda, pounding his gavel, handed down the decision: "Six crowns a month for Lars from Fishing Croft!"

The rap of the gavel was followed by various movements among the observers, the scraping of feet, coughing, and clearing of throats. Some agitation was evident in their facial expression.

As for Jon, he happened to recall something Father had said—that "boozing," or alcoholism, as he called it, was in many cases an illness.

A creaky masculine voice now announced that Isak from Myr Croft had "gone crazy."

Jon was startled at the expression. For him, it was a frightening concept, which he had only occasionally heard discussed at home, and then in hushed voices and with seriousness and compassion. The creaky voice had spat out the words as if he were saying casually the man was "bald" or had "caught a cold."

"His wife," the creaky voice continued, "wants thirty crowns a month to take care of him."

Jon grabbed Rickard's coat sleeve and was going to say something but stopped himself. The exchange of opinions around the black table continued.

"He's a terrible nut!" proclaimed a rotund, heavy district official, whom both Jon and Rickard knew as the innkeeper, Mr. Lund. It was rumored that he had money in the bank. "I know all about him, I do! It might help if he'd leave the bottle alone once in a while!"

Obviously, the innkeeper's comments were not in order, and he was reprimanded by a look from the chairman.

"Thirty crowns is an absolutely preposterous request!" Jansson from Heda began shuffling a pile of papers importantly, as if there might be supporting evidence for his statement among them.

Jon managed to whisper to Rickard, "But what about the hospital? If he's crazy, he should be put in the hospital, shouldn't he?"

"There isn't any . . . not here in the country district. Be quiet!"

Jansson from Heda had finished thumbing through his pile of papers.

"Let's cut it down to fifteen crowns. Do the members agree with me?"

"Yes! . . . Of course! . . . Quite right!"

The chairman's suggestion met with general approval. The Uddesund farmer's mouth twitched. The creaky-voiced man who had brought up the matter added to his plea by saying there were six minor children in Myr Croft, but this was greeted with stony silence.

Fifteen crowns!

The gavel fell. There was more clearing of throats, scraping of feet, and some low whispers.

A terrible feeling came over Jon. Only once before in his life had he experienced anything like this. One day he had chanced to peer into the waiting room at home in Soltuna and had seen a little girl with long curls, groping around strangely from the walls to the chairs to the tables. At length she seemed to be grasping at thin air, where-upon she fell to her hands and knees and began to crawl. At that moment it first struck Jon that the little girl was blind.

The same horror gripped him now. It was like the girl's groping about in a dark well, a boundless space, with nothing to get hold of.

New reports were presented at a fast clip. The voices growled and droned; most of those around the black table raised few objections; sums were announced, with raps of the gavel, in a steady stream.

It was as though Jon were battling in a place lacking both light and air. Still the afternoon sunbeams shone in through the windows, and the wide dusty bands seemed to settle on the heads of the members as if something menaced them from above. Jon felt, as he had a few moments before when he sought comfort in glancing at Rickard, that he somehow had to leave this land of terror and find a foothold in some tangible reality.

He turned his head in an attempt to see the people around him. They were adults. Jon looked up and, to his great astonishment, saw a familiar face.

The black slouch hat with its huge brim, the round, friendly face with cherubic cheeks, pince-nez glasses, the high white collar with the turned-down corners, the black scarf atop a vest with innumerable buttons—no, there was no mistake about it. Here was the biology teacher from school.

Jon lifted his school cap and bowed. Somewhat astonished, Rickard, who hadn't noticed the teacher, possibly because he was standing right behind the boys, did the same.

Both of them recalled the black bicycle leaning against the maple tree in the yard. Naturally! They had seen it every morning of the term at one of the side entrances to the school.

They both blushed. It was strange seeing someone here who belonged so thoroughly to the school world—in mid-July, right in the middle of the summer vacation.

The teacher from Soltuna lifted his hat and bowed with great dignity. A very proper man, he never had problems of discipline or inattentiveness in his classroom. His love of nature, especially plants and insects, was so strong that it was unfailingly transmitted to his pupils. It was because of him that the boys had searched the woods several days for *Pyrola umbellata,* a rare plant the teacher said should be growing there. To date, their search had been in vain.

This teacher conducted his lessons so simply and painstakingly that even those pupils who were not very quick-witted had time to formulate their answers. He reacted to sloppiness or a lack of diligence with a sense of deep personal sorrow.

All of this—plus butterflies of every color in the rainbow, wild animals of Africa, and Linnaeus's biological system—was at the back of their minds as the boys bowed and the teacher lifted his hat.

The decisions and the raps of the gavel on the table had ceased for a few minutes. Obviously, there had to be time out for getting new quids of tobacco and for wiping off damp foreheads with gaily patterned handkerchiefs.

"Well, do I see that my pupils are out enjoying themselves on this divinely ordained summer day?"

The teacher removed his pince-nez glasses. Two unusually clear blue eyes gazed nearsightedly at the world.

Since neither of the boys knew quite what to reply, they both remained silent.

Taking a yellow chamois from his vest pocket, the teacher began to polish his glasses.

"It could be," he went on, "it could be that this is a place of amusement for the various observers. You wouldn't be here otherwise. The miseries of your fellow men, coupled with their downfall, make your own lives more exciting, I would imagine. Pitiful sights often seem to be stimulating to people."

The teacher put his pince-nez glasses in place. From his

pocket he took out a longish red object, resembling a huge sausage. It looked like a scroll of fabric. He began to unroll it, slowly and methodically.

Fascinated, the boys watched his performance. At the same time, they listened to his words, which seemed calm and well chosen in comparison to the harsh, rasping voices of the participants in the meeting.

"For my part," the teacher said as he unrolled his sausage-like scroll, "this is the abode of sorrow. Sorrow, and the deterioration of mankind in general. Here bodies and souls are sold for the lowest possible amount. Here men conspire to exploit their fellow men—exploit them for their last drop of blood and spark of life."

By now the teacher had unrolled the huge rectangular red handkerchief almost to its last corner. Rickard and Jon waited with ever mounting curiosity as to what the final result would be. What could the teacher be concealing so carefully? Perhaps a beetle? Or a stone? Finally the last corner was exposed.

There was nothing to be seen.

Putting it to his face, he blew his nose so vehemently that the sound resembled a melancholy trumpet call.

He folded it again. Once more he began to roll it, and the sausage-like form grew. The boys continued to stare. The teacher said, "It disappoints me greatly to see two of my most beloved pupils enjoying this lovely God-given sunny day wallowing in other people's misery."

Rickard was completely perplexed. Jon gaped.

The teacher raised his finger and pointed at something, and the boys glanced in that direction.

Opposite the window in the District Council headquarters was a glass-windowed cabinet with green velvet curtains. Between the curtain and the glass was a sign whose legend, scrawled in red chalk, announced: THE DISTRICT LIBRARY.

"Here in this room," continued the delicate voice, "here in this room culture is contained within that cabinet over near the wall. It is, as you boys can plainly see, carefully locked so that nothing can slip out."

The teacher stuffed the long, red, sausage-like object into an invisible pocket beneath his coattail.

At that very same moment, the chairman rapped the gavel thunderously on the black table.

"Now we are going to hold an auction for five dependent persons!" he announced as silence fell across the room. "We'll begin with little Lovisa. Are you here, little Lovisa?"

No doubt about "little." A tiny, wizened old lady stepped up to the table and curtsied. Her hands were clasped beneath her checkered apron, and she gazed at the chairman with serious eyes. Over the years, he had been the decider of her fate—almost God the Father himself.

He regarded her with a certain measure of gracious benevolence. It was his responsibility to arrange matters for her in whatever way was best and cheapest for the district.

"A well-behaved, though silly woman," he said as he thrust his chin into the air. "Nice and well-mannered. It is never difficult for someone like this to be sold . . .

ahem . . . I mean, boarded out, actually. She was a found-
ling originally, but gentle as a lamb, you might say. She
can be very useful to you, too. Last year she not only
thinned out the turnips but also sowed potatoes, yes sir.
I assure you, it's worth a lot to get reliable help now that
workers are so expensive. The district will pay for her
room and board. Let's begin!"

"Ten crowns," shouted a prospective buyer from the
spirited clump of woodsmen, homeowners, and back-
porch sitters.

"Ten crowns . . . ten crowns . . ." the chairman repeated with a certain suspicious expression around his
mouth. "First bid, second bid, third bid. No one wants to
bid under?"

"Nine!"

The first bidder retorted.

"Seven, then, and I might add, not one öre less!"

But an old lady from one of the crofts, curiously enough
wearing a city hat, entered the bidding.

"I'll take five crowns for her!"

It was obvious from her voice that she was deeply embarrassed and utterly unaccustomed to speaking up in such
an awe-inspiring and totally masculine assembly.

"I must say," the chairman remarked gleefully, "that
was a very manly action from a woman! Going . . . going . . . gone! Sold! Sold!"

Jansson from Heda was lapsing into the role of auc-
tioneer more and more with each passing moment. It was a
matter of moving rapidly and speaking with sufficient volume so that the bidding would be brisker.

Shy and timid, little Lovisa went to join her new mistress, a red-faced woman who was adjusting her marketing hat.

At this point Rickard whispered in Jon's ear, "Well, at least that was a lucky break for old Lovisa. That lady is from Sage Fjeld. She lives alone, and there's almost surely twelve miles of wooded land between her and her nearest neighbor. She doesn't dare stay there by herself, you understand!"

Jansson from Heda now offered a small hunchbacked woman who was called Ida from Loss Home. No longer did he sound very compassionate. It turned out that this woman, too, was brought before the assembly every single year. She was too frail and infirm for anyone to really want her. She had cost the elders of the district a substantial amount of money to date. Still, the chairman attempted to gloss over these circumstances.

"Anyone with tiny children in the house can find good use for this woman! She's a corker at rocking the cradle!"

The miller laughed so uproariously that the rafters rang.

"You forgot to mention that she eats like a horse! I have had her in my house, and I know what I'm talking about!"

A slight commotion arose among the dependents in the corner over near the window. Jon looked over that way— and saw what he had so anxiously looked for earlier. He noticed a couple of thin childish legs in vigorous motion.

The owner of the legs suddenly got to the floor.

Jon heard the chairman's powerful voice in the background, chanting more than speaking. He didn't hear the outcome of the discussion about Ida from Loss Home. Poor Ida who looked so angular beneath her shawl, and yet she was reprimanded for eating too much.

He had concerns of his own. There was the boy—Alfrida's boy, the six-year-old, the one Mother had been so concerned about.

Father had declared that the days of the auctions were past, but he had been mistaken. Perhaps this was true in Soltuna and other larger cities and towns that had enough funds and enough feeling of responsibility to build homes for the poor and hospitals for the sick—But not here!

Jon felt lost.

With a chilling sensation along his spine and in his fingertips, he realized that at any moment it would be the little boy's turn. For him the district would not even need to offer a stipend. He could be useful to anyone who wanted him, to anyone who would himself pay for the boy in hard, cold cash.

With which of the villagers or crofters would he land? With Daniel from Vreta, the little farmer who looked like a fox and who, Jon had heard Soren say, was so stingy that he kept his own sons from going to school? Either they were needed at home or they could be sent to the fields in the southern part of Sweden where they could earn twelve öre per day.

Daniel stood right beside the boy. He seemed to be brushing against the lad with his long red nose.

And there on the other side was Alfrida. Why hadn't he recognized her earlier? Well, she was in her best Sunday clothing, of course, totally in black—black cape, black shawl, black skirt, black apron. Jon had never seen old Alfrida dressed this way before. Whenever she sold lace in the kitchens of Sand Cape, she wore light-colored clothing and a flowery apron—and high-buttoned shoes.

Jon recalled especially the high-buttoned shoes.

It was obvious that, out of respect for the assembly at the District Council headquarters, she had dressed as if she were going to the House of God, totally in black. The handkerchief, with which she quietly wiped her eyes, was white.

Father couldn't have dreamed what was to take place here.

Mother couldn't have known how it would all happen.

What in the world could Jon do when Jansson from Heda offered up Alfrida's boy? Would he be able to halt the proceedings of the District Council at their meeting?

Two other dependents had been assigned their homes for the coming year. The last was an old man, Mr. Krona, who for forty years—was it really possible that the man had worked for forty years, Jon and Rickard asked themselves —had served with a well-to-do farmer in Hedsel. By now he had gout and could no longer fulfill his obligations to the farmer. The farmer himself stood there and explained with some sorrow that he couldn't keep the man on in his service.

He was sold—for five crowns—to Mr. Lund the inn-keeper, who felt he could find some use for the man.

The farmer from Uddesund took the floor and asked if, after such a long and faithful period of service, his master couldn't provide for his remaining days in some other way, but no answer was forthcoming.

Jansson from Heda quickly tapped the gavel.

"Well, now, I guess we have only the little boy left. Here, Pelle. Come up and let the gentlemen take a look at you!"

Alfrida made a quick movement as if to smooth out the boy's hair, which was very fair and quite untidy; it stood straight up in the air, shaggy and unevenly cut.

Actually, he looked rather cocky. Naturally, he was strangely dressed in black pants that looked iridescent green in the most unexpected places. Both Jon and Rickard were well acquainted with this sort of garment— Rickard from experience. Jon had seen them on the elementary school boys in Soltuna. They had been made over out of suits, jackets, and topcoats that had been donated by rich people. They seemed stiff and were often hand sewn from whatever fabric was available.

The boy had on a striped shirt fastened with a high band around his neck, heavy woolen socks, and wooden shoes.

Pelle, as he seemed to be called, now did something rather curious. To be sure, on order from the chairman, he had stepped up to the table, but once there, he had unexpectedly sat down on a small stool, which he had held concealed behind his back.

Besides the councilmen, he was the only one in the room seated.

It all looked so comical that the observers began to giggle.

Jansson from Heda looked as if he were about to make some comment but was clearly in too much of a hurry. The meeting had dragged on for quite a long time.

"Pelle," he said in an official tone of voice, focusing his glance on the black pants and the child on the stool, "is fatherless and motherless. For six years, at the expense of the district, he has been boarded out with Alfrida from Ulvahult. As you can plainly see, he is healthy, well-developed, and large for his age."

Every eye in the room was on the boy seated on the stool. In the back rows, everyone stood on tiptoe, craning his neck. The boy still sat with his chin in the air. But his eyes sought out Alfrida over there by the window, and the corners of his mouth twitched.

The official voice continued.

"From this year on, Pelle can begin to make his own way. I can imagine that someone among this assembly would be willing to give a sum monthly to the parish to have him, for example, as a herder boy. In the winter he could carry wood and water, feed the chickens, or look after tiny children.

"The foster mother"—the chairman cleared his throat—"is of course unable to pay anything. Well, now, let me hear a bid."

"Oh!" Rickard whispered in Jon's ear. "I wouldn't have believed it could happen this way. Now our goose is cooked."

Jon grabbed Rickard's long jacket sleeve.

"We've got to do something! Look at Alfrida; she's crying! And he's so little. Mother and Father . . ."

Daniel from Vreta—the man with the pinched nose—stepped up a couple of paces and bid six crowns.

"The only thing to do," Rickard said softly into Jon's ear, "the only thing to do is to bid—more than what they bid."

"If only Father had been here . . ." Jon said with parched lips.

"Yes, *if* only he had!"

At that point Jon looked up at Rickard. He recognized that old, peculiar note in Rickard's voice, and suddenly his forehead was burning.

A faint smile was on Rickard's face—at once guileless and, at least it seemed to Jon, contemptuous. Generally, he looked like that when he let something slip out about "the rich people."

Another voice was heard from the group along the side wall.

"I bid eight crowns!"

Jon and Rickard stood on tiptoe.

The bid had come from a small man who looked energetic but gruff. After he had entered his bid, he took his drooping mustache, put it in his mouth, and sucked on it.

"The shopkeeper from Hedsel!" Rickard whispered.

That was so far away. Alfrida would almost certainly never see the boy again.

"Father will come down here tomorrow," Jon whispered to Rickard, feverishly and rather loudly. "The minute he hears about this, he'll come down and straighten things out!"

Rickard turned his head. He looked Jon straight in the eye, and Jon didn't blink. He said aloud, "When Jansson's gavel comes down, everything will be decided, don't you see? Tomorrow it too late!"

5

Pyrola Umbellata

RICKARD had spoken so loudly that people began to look quizzically in the direction of the two boys.

Even Jansson from Heda turned his head to restore order. He waved his gavel threateningly in the air.

Daniel from Vreta glared at the shopkeeper from Hedsel.

"Nine crowns," he offered reluctantly, grouchily.

"Going . . ." said the chairman, thinking he had received an unexpectedly fine bid. "Going . . ."

"Ten!"

The word came like a shot.

Jon stared unwaveringly and despairingly at Jansson from Heda. Had he heard correctly? Was it quite clear that he understood Jon was bidding?

Jon himself felt that he had sounded like a dynamite explosion—but who could tell? Maybe no one had heard him. It was like a bad dream where you shout and shout but can't make a sound!

Anyway, Rickard had heard. He grabbed Jon's jacket sleeve and whispered.

"Great, Jon! Just keep it up. We can sell shrimp to the military installations near Hedsel for five öre each and . . . and shoot crows, because there's a twenty-five öre bounty on them!"

"Who, might I ask," queried the chairman as people craned their necks and the boy Pelle turned clear around on his stool, "who is it that entered the bid?"

"I did."

Something began to click inside Jon. Finally, he had managed to say "I did" so that it was audible.

Sternly, Jansson from Heda observed the boys. He pulled at the mustache, which reached almost to his jaw.

At that point the Uddesund farmer was heard. "That's Doctor Halvorsson's boy bidding for his father—the Soltuna doctor who's substituting for Dr. Liljenstam. He's entitled to a vote here. The boy is bidding for his father."

"Are you bidding for your father, son?"

"Yes, I am. He couldn't come here today because he's out on sick calls."

Jon swallowed. He had done it—he had bid for his father. He knew he had bid for his father even if he hadn't yet asked Father.

Dead silence reigned among those close to him. Alfrida's white handkerchief had come to rest. No longer was she shifting it from eye to eye.

Jansson from Heda looked doubtful and disturbed. He had great respect for medical men. In addition, he was painfully aware that he had been able to shove the auction of dependents through simply because the provincial doctor, Liljenstam, was in the hospital and couldn't poke his nose into the matter. And what a fortunate coincidence! The minister had gone to officiate at a burial in Hedsel and couldn't put in his two cents' worth either.

Those troublesome boys!

There would be so much talk, so many comments. And the worst thing of all might happen—the *Soltuna Daily News* might get wind of the auction.

It could turn into a huge mess.

The best thing was to get it over and done with. The press and the medical profession were the up and coming things these days—much more dangerous to a man of the future than the old shopkeeper from Hedsel.

"I would like a word," a soft voice said from somewhere

right behind Jon and Rickard, "I want to attest, to confirm the recent declaration made by my pupil, Jon Halvorsson. My name is Mr. Ryd, and I'm a teacher from the Soltuna Consolidated Latin School. This pupil is qualified in every respect to represent his father, Doctor Halvorsson. Naturally, he's not of age, but unforeseen circumstances dictate that his declaration will have to be considered as coming from one of age."

"Ten crowns are bid," the chairman repeated. Hastily, he cast a glance at Daniel from Vreta and toward the corner where the tradesman from Hedsel sucked on his straggling mustache.

It was almost unthinkable that someone would dare to bid against a provincial doctor and a man in the field of education. The muted voice of the teacher, without much volume to it, seemed to reach every corner of the room, even the cracks in the floor.

Daniel from Vreta put a hand behind his one good ear.

"Going, going, gone!"

The gavel came down.

Fair-haired Pelle got up, grabbed his stool, and fled, clacking his wooden shoes, to join Alfrida over by the windowsill. He buried his face in the old lady's black apron. Laughter, whispers, and general stirrings among the observers and bidders followed his hasty flight.

The Uddesund farmer, unbuttoning his coat, put his thumbs in the armholes of his huge vest and leaned back in his chair, making the chair legs creak. He stared at Jansson from Heda, who hastily declared the meeting adjourned.

Rickard felt a hand being placed lightly on his shoulder.

It remained there in a gentle grip, steering him through the mob of people over to the door.

Out in the yard beneath the huge maple tree, they remained standing—the teacher and the two boys. The chairman, the observers, and the bidders mingled with the groups of women waiting anxiously outside. The big topic of conversation was not difficult to make out. Everyone was stealing glances at the three under the maple, and a couple of little children rushed up and stared unashamedly.

Jansson from Heda walked by with the bundle of papers under his arm. He looked straight over the heads of the crowd as if his high position forbade him to lower his eyes to the scum of the earth, but Jon noticed that he tugged nervously at his whiskers as he passed the teacher.

Removing his cap, Jon wiped his forehead with a clean handkerchief, which, thanks to Mari, could always be found in his pocket. Then he handed it to Rickard.

The teacher said, "I would like to beg the pardon of my pupils. I have committed a serious error. It seemed to me scarcely believable that my pupils could be at a meeting of the Public Assistance Commission with anything but curiosity and enjoyment in mind. But I was mistaken. I realize now that all was in order and that Jon's father had arranged everything."

Jon, feeling that he had to make some comment, mumbled, "Mother and Father."

"Yes, of course. A very harmonious blend. I would like to add"—the teacher's hand left Rickard's shoulder as he straightened his pince-nez glasses—"I would like to add that I support young Svensson's point of view. Tomorrow would have been too late. The chairman, Mr. Jansson, was doubtless certain he was improving the district's economic status. As for myself, I am here on a mission for a friend of mine, the editor of the *Soltuna Daily News*. My errand is to give him a written report on what has happened here."

As thoughtfully as if he had been sitting at his desk in the classroom and were systematically reciting his lessons, Rickard said unexpectedly, "We have you to thank, Mr. Ryd. I was afraid for a while that Jansson from Heda would ask Jon for some sort of written proof from his father. But I guess he didn't dare."

"I notice," replied the teacher, "that my pupils are good friends. I guess you are spending the summer vacation together. I'm still concerned that I did my pupils a grave injustice. If our plans coincide, it would give me great pleasure to show you the place in the Vidinge woods where *Pyrola umbellata* is at present in full bloom. Perhaps they're a bit faded, but I'm certain there are several examples suitable for pressing. I'll come down to Sand Cape" —the teacher had taken out a notebook, which the boys knew well from the classroom—"let me see—Saturday, about one o'clock. Would that be convenient for you?"

Removing their caps, Jon and Rickard thanked the teacher. The teacher made a note. Then he shook hands with both of them and grabbed his black bicycle. They watched him push it out through the crowd of people and through the gate leading out to the village road.

6

Three Boys Are Happy

A BREEZE, with a hint of evening chill to it, wafted through the treetops. Jon and Rickard sighed with relief. It had been quite a strain. They straightened their school caps. They were well aware that they were the center of general attention. Rickard voiced their feelings.

"Hey, Jon, let's get out of here, quick."

They had been so occupied talking to Mr. Ryd that they hadn't noticed two persons approaching them.

"Mr. Jon, here's Pelle. And . . . and God bless you, Mr. Jon, and your father!"

Their troubles weren't over. Before them stood Alfrida and Pelle.

Jon began to blush slowly from his neck clear up to his forehead as the meaning of the old lady's words dawned on him.

"Here in this bundle is his sweater and a change of underwear. I've tried to take care of him as best I could, poor as I am. And the stool. I'm sorry to tell you that he and the stool are inseparable. He takes it everywhere he goes. And, Mr. Jon, will you greet your mother—what a good soul she is—and tell her that I regret I haven't much to send with the child but that I'll be at Sand Cape next week with a couple of bunches of lace, which I'll give to her as a thank offering, knowing the boy will have a good home!"

Alfrida curtsied a number of times as she spoke. When she had finished, her mouth was set in a straight line. The boys noticed that her cheeks, from which all color had gone, were wet. She had reached the moment of separation.

On close examination it turned out that Pelle had huge, round blue eyes, which, without blinking, he focused on the boys. He pressed the seat of his stool against his stomach, holding the four round legs defensively against the outside world.

"Oh, but"—said Jon, gazing from the old lady to the boy —"but that isn't the way it's supposed to be at all. We . . . Mother and Father . . . didn't have anything like this in mind. They're only interested in having Pelle stay with Alfrida."

The old lady looked very confused. Pelle directed the legs of the stool straight at Jon.

Rickard broke in.

"Jon means that the doctor will help you and that he'll see to it that the ten crowns per month are paid to the district. But Pelle can stay with you."

"Just like before," Jon added by way of explanation. "Nothing will be changed, Miss Alfrida. He can still stay with you at Ulvahult."

Jon was perspiring mightily.

Alfrida stared at him. Her tightly pursed lips opened and closed a couple of times, but no words came out. Finally, she said, "Mr. Jon is good. He and his parents are fine people. But, Mr. Jon, you have bought Pelle, and Pelle has to go and live in your house. We'll see about it later. The doctor can decide. But it wouldn't be right for me to take the boy away with me now. What would the Public Assistance Commission say? What would all the others standing around here say?"

Alfrida gestured toward the yard where groups of curious onlookers were still standing around. Poor, deformed Ida from Loss Home was just passing through the gate. Wagons with fine horses hitched to them rolled around the school property, but it never occurred to any of the farmers to offer her a ride. No doubt she had been auctioned to people who themselves stood on the threshold of poverty and couldn't afford the luxury of a carriage.

Rickard's eyes followed her for a long while. He knew more about the district than Jon did. It was a sure thing that the crippled creature would have to make her way on foot to the mountainous district over seldom trodden, even occasionally nonexistent, paths.

Rickard clasped his hands.

Suddenly, he caught sight of Daniel from Vreta and noticed that he was glaring menacingly at Jon.

Hastily, Rickard said, "Listen, Jon, I think Alfrida is right. It will look a little strange if we don't take the boy with us."

Jon was of two minds about Pelle. But it did occur to him that Mother would probably be delighted to see the little boy she had been so worried about—see him in the flesh, happy and contented, come wandering up the veranda steps. Mother loved children so much—all children. Also, it was necessary for Father and Alfrida to come to an agreement as to how the payment due the district was to be arranged. They could take care of these matters when Alfrida came to get Pelle.

"Well, we'll take him with us for the time being. Miss Alfrida, can you come over to Sand Cape this evening and discuss things with my mother and father?"

Alfrida curtsied and nodded.

"I'll come as soon as I've milked Sippa," she said, not taking her eyes from Pelle's fair tuft of hair. This time she dared to reach out her hand and smooth it. She handed the bundle of Pelle's clothing to Rickard before she de-

parted with quick little steps. You couldn't see her feet below her long black skirt. No one spoke to her. She was known as a person who kept very much to herself, Miss Alfrida. Poor she was, to be sure, and her Ulvahult home had no more than one cow and one pig, but she had been born into good, respectable farming stock.

Rickard and Jon didn't linger.

"Come on, Pelle!" Rickard said as he poked the boy in the side. "We'll clear out of here before someone comes along and eats you up!"

Pelle, holding his stool even more tightly, had to half run to keep up.

But as they rounded the schoolhouse corner and were out of sight of the curious assembly in the yard, he began to giggle unexpectedly.

"Eat me up! Eat me up! There isn't anybody who can eat me up, either!"

"You never know about these things ahead of time. Pelle! Your hair looks just like the hair on the small goats up at Vidinge!"

They slackened their pace, and all three began to laugh.

Jon felt relieved. Rickard had no difficulty getting onto an easy footing with other boys, even those who were younger than he. It was like that at school, where he was often asked to help guide the younger pupils in games and gym. Jon had a hard time with such matters. He felt awkward and stupid and consequently looked that way fairly often.

How wonderful it was to be out under the blue sky

again! Here honeyed smells wafted from the yards, from elderberries and lavender and newly mown hay. The coo of the doves echoed from both sides of the road, from the birches in the plowed fields where magpies and thrushes called out good evening to one another from the treetops.

The harvest workers were on the way home. You could hear them talking and laughing on the other side of the pasture.

Rickard said, "We're going to run into them. Ugh, Jon!"

They looked toward the curve in the road that was dusty and almost white in the burning July heat. The westering sun was shining on the road.

Jon caught the meaning of Rickard's words. The harvest workers were mainly young people, happy at the thought that the day's work was over. They would be curious at meeting the three boys and would ask questions and make jokes.

Jon felt he had seen enough of mankind for a good while to come.

"We could cut off here," he suggested, pointing, "and sneak down directly to the shore. There's no path through the woods, of course, but it will be cooler there than out here in the fields, and if we can only get to the water, it won't be difficult to find our way after that."

Between a potato patch and a grain field was a small ditch with a barely perceptible path on one bank.

Rickard was quick-thinking. "We could go for a swim. Jon, I'd give a million for a dip right now."

The voices of the harvesters were coming closer.

"Let's get going!" Rickard whispered. "Pelle, run between us!"

Once again they ran. First came Rickard with the bundle, followed by Pelle with the stool clutched to his chest, and finally Jon almost crouching. Pelle had a long torso and little short legs, but they worked like drumsticks. The boys had a feeling they were being hunted down and knew it was best to get as far from the District Council headquarters as they could with the utmost speed.

Had they kept to the country road as before, they would have reached the edge of the woods more rapidly. This way they had to make their way on the headland over barren slopes piled with gray rocks, where there were clumps of juniper bushes that resembled the groups of people in the yard of the district headquarters.

Creeping vines covered the hill, which at a distance looked blue in the heat. The ground was parched, and in the small gulleys drooped dusty clumps of nettles. But masses of violet heather covered the crowns and hollows.

They headed toward the big woods. Once there, they would be secure. The woods would provide good cover.

Rickard thought of an old proverb that Per-Anders often recited almost reverently: "The forest is the home of the poor and the fur coat of the crofter."

There were aspens and hazel trees with white clusters, bluebells and wild chervil. There was sure to be an underground spring nearby because here and there soft green grass grew.

In among the pines all was calm, just as they had expected.

"Well, it can't be far to Vidar Lake from here," Rickard said, turning to Jon, who answered with a nod. "It's great to get out of the heat of the sun. What do you say, Pelle?"

The boy didn't respond, but for the first time he shifted his stool and put it under his arm.

"Let's catch our breath for a bit," Jon suggested. "Hey, look, there are blueberries here. Have you ever seen such big ones? It's because of the blueberries that I know this part of the woods. Mari usually comes here every summer. She says the biggest berries grow here."

The huge berries dangled like misty dark blue drops from an umbrella. The boys stopped picking them one at a time and started gathering them in handfuls, stuffing their mouths full.

"You sure can get thirsty in that damned hole of a district house," Rickard remarked. His fingers were dripping with blueberry juice.

Jon looked askance at Pelle. He suspected that even a word such as "damned" was unknown in Alfrida's Ulvahult.

But Pelle seemed undisturbed. Not only were his fingers blue, but also his ears and his hair.

Rickard observed him critically.

"That dip in the lake," he remarked, "is going to prove to be necessary."

Pelle giggled. It seemed he was accustomed to begin whatever he was about to say with a giggle.

"Dip? In the lake? Are we going for a swim?"

In the midst of the blueberry patch, he stood there with his legs wide apart and with eyes so big and astonished that Jon was filled with suspicion.

"Don't you usually take a dip in the lake?" he queried. "Ulvahult runs clear down to Vidar Lake. Lovely, round flat stones . . ."

"Never done it," Pelle said.

Both Jon and Rickard drew themselves up and began to speak almost simultaneously.

"You mean you've never had a swim in the lake? Why not?"

And Rickard added, "Are you afraid of the water?"

"Alfrida says that swimming in cold water is very dangerous. You can get T.B. that way, she says."

Rickard and Jon exchanged glances. Tuberculosis was the most dreaded of all ailments among the local populace —a disease that every year claimed thousands of lives in Sweden.

"You don't get tuberculosis from swimming in cold water," Jon explained. "You get it if you're undernourished and if you don't keep yourself clean. Instead, it makes you healthy to swim."

"The other day I read in the *Soltuna Daily News* that tuberculosis is believed to be spreading among the children in the schools. *Science*"—somehow Rickard made the word sound long and weighty and important—"*science* has begun to *come to the conclusion* that tuberculosis is spread through contamination."

With open mouth, Jon stood and listened. It happened

more and more frequently that Rickard was informed about all sorts of things because he read the newspaper. Naturally, he didn't buy them himself, but Per-Anders brought home bundles of discarded newspapers to wrap his eggs in. Rickard was in charge of packing the eggs, but before doing so, he would read the newspapers in the chicken house.

Pelle was completely unconcerned over the long, difficult words. But still he stared, first at Jon and then at Rickard.

"Are you going to let me swim? In the lake? Today? Right now? With you?"

He scarcely breathed between questions. They seemed to pour out.

Simultaneously Rickard and Jon, standing there in the blueberry patch looking down at Alfrida's boy in his striped shirt and the greenish-black, strangely constructed pants, realized that he regarded them as heroes, as almost gods. Since his birth he had lived alone with an elderly, superstitious woman in a solitary croft in the big woods. His physical needs had been provided for by the woman to the best of her ability, but it was clear the child had hardly ever had any fun out of life!

Rickard pushed his school cap down over his ears and held one hand out to Pelle.

"We'll take a swim. You can bet your life we'll take a swim. Come on. Let's get going!"

Once more they started through the woods, which grew thicker and thicker. They ran over golden moss and climbed over windfallen trees, where dry branches crackled underfoot. They came to swampy ground, where swarms of gnats hung in buzzing, misty clouds in the air; they came to small meadows, where grazing livestock herds had left hoofprints in the broken ground and huge cowpaths between the grassy hillocks; they ran across peat moss and brooks with white foam on their surfaces.

At first Jon had been a little surprised when Rickard, leaving the blueberry patch, had set his course in among the pines. As for himself, he would have chosen to run farther off to the left. But in the woods Rickard was clearly in command. It was obvious that he had gotten to know his way around the country since living with Per-Anders and helping out at Uddesund. His sense of direction was sharp; he relied on the position of the sun and was used to territory that was rugged and almost impossible to penetrate.

Jon realized, too, that it really didn't matter if they ran obliquely down to the lake instead of following a straight course. Certainly, Rickard knew what he was doing, and no harm would come if they approached Vidar Lake closer to Sand Cape. The shore was rocky and hard to get across and would be especially so for Pelle in his wooden shoes.

Jon followed both the others without stopping to give the matter further thought.

7

Adventure with the Herders

IT would have been nice if there had been a path to follow. Rickard and Jon were both on the lookout for one. You might have thought the farmers' oxen, cows and heifers, sheep and goats, who were usually herded up through the woods, would have trampled paths down to the water this hot summer, but they discovered none.

Jon searched between the tree trunks for the first welcome glimpse of blue water, but in vain. In fact, he began to feel that they were going upward at an unusual rate. Steeper and steeper was their path. They had to climb over rocks and crawl through thickets so tight that their hands and faces were scratched with brambles.

"Look out, Pelle," Jon warned him. "Watch that you don't get a branch in your eye!"

He had heard of a boy who had gone astray in the woods and had lost an eye that way.

Startled grouse flew up from the heather and, in turn, startled the boys with their noise as they burst from cover.

"Elks!" Rickard said as he pointed at some droppings in a crevice.

"I just don't understand this," Jon said thoughtfully. "We must be right in the middle of the big woods leading up to the mountains. By now we should have caught sight of the lake, shouldn't we?"

With his head tipped backward, Rickard looked up at the endless blue sky above the tops of the firs.

"Yes, I guess we're a little off course," he admitted, "but that's no great tragedy. Let's climb up a little bit farther. In a while I can climb one of the tall firs, once we get high enough, and get my bearings. I can't help but see Vidar Lake. For that matter, doesn't it look lighter over there? Aren't the woods thinning out?"

Pelle, who for a moment had looked a little worried, began to giggle.

Rickard inspired confidence and trust. He was so sure-footed in the worst terrain, and he spoke consolingly. What he said must be right.

At this point he spotted a light green grove before them. What could it be? Meadowland, perhaps?

Heading for the light green patch, they ducked beneath branches and pushed forward, but it wasn't a little grove. It was a broad path in the woods, trampled down by hundreds of hoofs.

"This is . . ." Rickard began, but said no more. All three stood stock still.

Forests are still the domain of danger and adventure. To be sure, the woods furnish a shield against the whisperings of men, their glances, and their falsehoods. But it is quite clear within the forest that all creatures, from the smallest insect nestling in the pine needles or the moss to lynxes, roe, and elk, live and fight for their very existence. There is the joy of living, but there is also the threat to life. A summer day dies away and night falls. Autumn nights were not far away, and winter was not too remote, either, with its deadly cold.

"Elks?" Rickard thought, whereupon he instinctively grabbed Jon, who had ventured out onto the path, pulling him back into the protective shield of the trees once more.

The path was so straight that they realized it had been created by animals completely unconcerned with any hindrance, who had pushed forward, shoving aside any barriers or breaking them down. This part of the path was illuminated by sunlight, but farther down it was swallowed by the woods and then was lost in a deep valley. Upward it led across slopes, ridges, and mountain ledges, almost directly up to the sky. Straight and open it was, and there wasn't a sign of life anywhere. But a thundering noise was coming from further up. The din was beyond belief.

"Thunder?" Jon wondered aloud.

"The God of the Forest!" Pelle suggested. "Or the Great Horse. Or maybe the Great Black Pig!"

Alfrida had told him stories about these three dwellers in the woods.

Actually, it sounded as if all three of them were on the way from the Hedsel mountains and slopes down the forest path.

Pelle placed the stool against his stomach once again, hiding himself behind the protective backs of the bigger boys.

A cracking noise came from above—as sharp as the cracks when the military troops had target practice at the installation at Hedsel.

The earth thundered, and other noises blended into the din—bellowing and bleating, boisterous and tumultuous.

And there at the top where the forest path joined the horizon, the three astonished boys saw something utterly amazing. The ridge seemed to be moving in waves and, what was even worse, the thickets and bushes seemed to have come to life. They bristled and moved.

From every imaginable direction, livestock emerged.

Hosts of horns swept back and forth as they entered the path. The oxen and cows had bundles of twigs fastened to their horns so that they could more easily drive away the flies. This made it seem that the bushes themselves had begun to move and rustle down the slopes.

More and more animals trotted onto the path. Sheep and goats joined the cattle. It became increasingly crowded between the pines, and the noise grew by the minute.

Not only were the animals themselves causing a din with the tramping of hundreds of hoofs, with bellows and bleats. There were their bells that jingled and jangled. The herders who drove them weren't very large in stature, but they could still create plenty of noise. Cracking their long whips, they laughed and shouted and blew their trumpets and cow horns.

Cautiously, Rickard, Jon, and Pelle withdrew to the shade of the pines.

"This is the village livestock being driven home from the outlying territory," Rickard whispered. "These are the herders I've told you about before, Jon. Did you ever see the like of them? How they can take such responsibility as small as they are, I don't know!"

By now they could see the bell-cow in the lead, not far away. She trotted along at an even pace. The oxen were making the homeward journey peacefully, and the sheep, with their lambs at their sides, flocked together in billowing gray groups.

But the heifers and goats—and there were many—knew how to cause their herders trouble. All that was needed to create disorder and chaos was for one of them to stray from

83

the path or break up a flock of more peaceful animals. The livestock would spread in all directions, and the herders would blow and bellow and throw sticks and stones after them.

Timidly, Pelle pressed his nose against a wide, shielding tree.

Everything—the huge horns of the oxen and rams, the unceasing noise, but most of all the people herding the animals—frightened him. They were only children, but many of the boys were as big and sturdy as bears. There was no mistaking the strength in their arms and the fact that they were constantly on the alert. Their eyes never wandered from their herds, and their ears were always listening.

The girls, too, had developed both muscular strength and agility, and their shouted talk was as loud as that of the boys. They looked poor and ragged, all of them, wearing straw hats, carrying food sacks in their hands, and wearing sundials on strings around their necks.

It occurred to Pelle, to his horror, that this was the fate he had just escaped at the meeting of the Public Assistance Commission. He took still another step backward in among the trees, stumbled on a branch, and fell down.

Rickard jerked to attention. He knew that this group from the villages of the Vidinge district had a rather bad reputation. The herders, with very few exceptions, were youngsters who were "very much at home with all the vices," as the expression went—orphaned at an early age and toughened by hard work. Very early in life they learned to use their fists. Banding together—and here there were about twenty of them—they could be quite a threat to anyone around, often egging one another on, confident of safety in numbers.

Rickard knew that it would be just as well if none of the herders observed the three of them seeking shelter beneath the branches. But Pelle's hasty fall unfortunately attracted the attention of one of the herder boys who happened to be hunting for a pair of runaway goats in among the trees.

The boy stopped and stared at Pelle as if he didn't believe his eyes. Actually, this was an unexpected sight in the big woods—a little fellow with a stool in his arms. The boy, guessing that the child could hardly have landed there alone, looked around searchingly. He caught sight of Jon and Rickard. The first thing he noticed was the school crest on Jon's school cap.

The herder boy wasn't any more than ten or twelve years old, but he was sun- and wind-burned, and his straw hat dangled at the back of his neck. His eyes gazed shrewdly from beneath a tuft of dark hair. He was a bit different from the other herders in that he wasn't wearing a shirt and pants but instead a long robe, which made him look like a miniature priest. He was barefooted. The skin on his feet, insofar as it was visible under layers of dust and dirt, seemed like leather.

At this moment he let out a whistle that rose above all the other noises. His comrades responded immediately. They came up curiously, one after the other, to see what was going on. A couple of the smallest merely cast shy glances at the group along the edge of the path, then wandered in among the thick vegetation where the goats had disappeared.

But the others stood and stared, and part of the noise ceased. The livestock, no longer being driven along, stopped. The bell-cow had found a patch of pastureland.

The boy in the priestly robe said, in a rough voice, "Well, what attractive strangers we have in the woods!" His tone of voice was anything but friendly.

And matters grew worse.

One of the large girl herders, wearing a torn, tattered skirt that reached to the ground, eagerly broke in. "Hey, that's Pelle from Ulvahult. I know. He's the one that was supposed to be sold at the District Council headquarters on Thursday!"

"Thursday," another of the girls said insolently. She was pretty and blue-eyed, with hair as fair as angel's hair. "Thursday, Thursday, big fat hen; Thursday, Thursday, once again."

The large girl, with two long brown pigtails dangling from her tattered straw hat, chanted the words over and over, obviously in a mood to fight.

"Are you the ones who bought the little kid? You harpies! What do you think you're going to do with the poor boy?"

Jon and Rickard merely stood there, not saying a word. The animal smells hit them in waves. Both of them had experienced attacks of this sort—and not infrequently at that—when the Latin School pupils from Soltuna encountered the gang from the public school. Immediately, they were aware that they had made a serious mistake wearing their school caps here in the woods. They were caste symbols, so to speak. But both had needed their hands free to push their way through the thickets, besides which Rickard was carrying the little bundle of Pelle's clothing. It had been more convenient to wear their caps on their heads.

At the tone of the girl's voice, Pelle stuck the legs of his stool in Rickard's back. His eyes filled with terror as he saw more and more of the herders gathering around them.

Jon attempted to discuss matters calmly.

"We did not buy Pelle," he said. "We're just boys ourselves. He . . ."

He got no further. One of the herders, a small, muscular, dwarf-like person—the type who enjoys playing the clown in front of his comrades—suddenly bellowed like a bull, quite realistically. At the same time, he sprang through the air and grabbed Jon's school cap.

Pelle was scared to death. With his stool in front of his face as a shield, he fled in among the trees and disappeared.

At that moment a heifer sauntered straight across the path, and an entire flock of sheep scattered, separated, and went off in every direction.

"Little Anna's animals are heading for the marshes!"

A couple of the girls rushed, as fast as their legs would carry them, across the path and into the wooded area on the other side.

The boy in the priest's robe yelled, "You may be good at the books, but that's all you can do! Among us people all you can do is disturb our flocks and create chaos."

No elementary school pupil in Soltuna would have dared to shout at Rickard in that fashion. There, "Svensson's boy" was known and highly respected. Naturally, his father was a boozer . . . but his brothers were greatly feared.

None of the herders here knew him. What they imagined was that here were a couple of the detested "cats" from the Latin School who, if one were to judge from the circumstances, had kidnaped a boy unable to care for himself, almost certainly with the most evil purposes in mind. Jon's spindly figure inspired no respect. Rickard seemed more muscular, but among this group he didn't exactly impress them as a killer.

The herder in the priest's robe looked as if he were sucking on something. Suddenly, he spat at Jon's face. That is to say, he aimed at Jon's face but hit Jon's collar.

"For that you can go to the devil," Rickard said.

His expression and tone of voice were those of a boy from the tenement district on Quarry Road, not of a pupil at the Latin School. The herders looked a little bewildered. Had they judged him wrongly?

"Did you have something else to say, you louse?" piped up the fellow who was acting the clown.

The priest-boy, moving his angular shoulder, shoved Rickard. At the same moment, Rickard thrust out his left fist, quick as lightning. The blow hit the other fellow above one ear, and since he was unprepared for an attack

with such strength behind it, he fell down on all fours. The circle of herders crowded closer and closer around their antagonists.

"Run, Jon!" Rickard shouted commandingly. "Run and find Pelle! Otherwise, he'll get lost. I'll take care of things here! Run, please!"

Jon wasn't a coward. During the first year at the Latin School, he had learned a trick or two from Rickard, who knew almost everything there was to know about fighting. In addition, Jon was agile and quick. Generally, he didn't shy away from a fight.

It wasn't fear that made him obey Rickard's command.

It was a fleeting thought that the mention of Pelle's name had brought to mind. Just imagine! The important adults in the community had intended to make a herder boy out of Pelle, with his innocent eyes, blue as the sky, and his tuft of fair hair. If they had succeeded, would he,

like these youngsters, have turned into a fighting-mad animal with cunning, angry eyes? Had these rough, unpleasant girls ever been gentle little ones? Had the boys ever
resembled Pelle some years back?

Jon wished that Rickard had never laid hands on the
boy in the long robe, no matter how much he deserved it.
Some of the herders were certainly older than both Rickard and himself, but still—you never fought with someone
smaller or with anyone deformed. These people seemed to
be a combination of both.

Unmoved by the shower of taunts and raw epithets that
accompanied him, Jon disappeared into the woods to look
for Pelle. He wasn't in the least worried about Rickard.
Rickard, he knew, was equal to any situation where flexi-
bility and strength were decisive.

The herders now experienced this at first hand.

The priest-boy got to his feet again and removed his
long robe. Beneath it his torso was bare. His only other
garment was a pair of ragged knickers.

Quite in command of the situation, Rickard waited.

The girls yelled, "Get him, Father Priest, get him!"

One of the boys, eager to fight, flew treacherously at
Rickard from the side at the very moment the priest-boy
stumbled to his feet, waving his fists furiously.

Rickard Svensson, trained among the hooligans in Soltuna, didn't budge an inch. He hit the newcomer squarely
in the stomach with his foot.

These youngsters, wild though they were, still had their
own unwritten laws. As Rickard was attacked, the rank

and file shouted, "One fights against one; two fight against the devil!"

The battle, then, turned out to be between the two original contestants, Rickard and the priest-boy, and this was actually better than Rickard had hoped for.

It was almost too easy for him. The herder boy was strong, to be sure, with arms as big as poles, but he had never been trained in any of the fine points of fighting.

Rickard boxed for a while, but then, without further ado, he used a trick he had learned from his older brother —the one who had spent much of his eventful youth at sea.

Suddenly, the herder boy found himself falling, his legs crumpling beneath him. Quick as a wink, Rickard straddled his shoulder. He pressed the boy's face into the dry moss, which they had tramped down in the course of their brief fight.

The outcome of the combat was undeniably disgrace, and the cries of encouragement from the onlookers had died down. In among the pines, you could still hear the youngest herders hunting for the strays.

Rickard looked around the circle without saying a word. He had no hope of being able to talk sensibly with these half-wild children. To make his point perfectly clear, he again rubbed his enemy's face in the dirt. When the boy struggled once more to his feet, his eyes were swollen, and both his nose and forehead were bleeding.

"Go wash yourself off when you come to a brook," Rickard advised as he brushed the knees of his trousers and picked up the bundle of Pelle's clothing and Jon's school cap. He had pushed his own down over his ears in a gesture of defiance, and there it had remained all during the proceedings.

He kept his eyes on the group to see if anyone else wanted to take him on, but nobody moved.

It was just possible that the boy in the long robe, who was now glumly putting this strange garment back on, was the strongest in the bunch—the leader.

If that were true, there was nothing more to be said.

"You'd be wise to help the little ones with their livestock," Rickard remarked dryly. "Evening is falling fast, and the marshland isn't far from here. And don't start a fight again because you aren't the strongest fellow in the world!"

His words and movements were entirely confident and fearless, commanding perhaps more respect even than the recent victory.

After all, he was still surrounded by enemies armed with clubs and whips, and there was no guarantee that their unwritten laws could be trusted.

But the circle of herders around him seemed to open willingly, and Rickard sauntered calmly and impassively away under the pines, where Pelle and Jon had disappeared earlier.

For a little while, he followed the forest path, since he was curious to know how quickly the herders would be able to gather their flocks and begin to drive them again. To his surprise, it took only a short time. There were no shouts or sounds of the horns as there had been before, since the defeat had dampened their spirits. The herders were tired after a long, hot day, but to his surprise Rickard heard them begin singing and recognized the song as one he and Jon had once upon a time learned in the Misses Martells' Private School. The teacher had told them a romantic tale about the little herders who tended their sheep and lambs in the beautiful woods.

Reality, as it often turned out, was something else again.

> "The evening fast is falling;
> My flocks their sleep require,
> My mother waits to see me,
> And food is on the fire.
> The bells will soon be ringing
> And sunset time is here;
> I'll soon be sleeping soundly;
> The dark of night is near.
> Hurry, now, and don't delay.
> Night takes over from the day."

Rickard picked up a pine cone from the ground and threw it against a tree so hard that the trunk seemed to sing.

8

The Swim

As if drawn in charcoal, a gigantic pine on the mountain towered against a multicolored sky—lilac, white, blue, and violet. Rickard recognized the tree. From his skiff on the lake, he had often seen it rising in solitary majesty above the ridge. In clear weather its silhouette was even visible from Kalv Island.

He needed to climb only a little more than halfway up its huge trunk to get his bearings. There was Vidar Lake spreading out in shiny blueness, with a darkening cove nearby. Happily, Rickard slid unhurriedly down to the ground.

With long, decisive steps he moved down the rolling meadows toward the shore. He knew that Jon, once he had found Pelle, would also head for the lake, where it would be easier for them to find one another. His calculations were correct. The cove was a narrow, tapering thrust of water, running in toward the mountain. Almost immediately he could spot them down by the shore.

One of them, standing expectantly, let out a shrill whistle, which might well have been intended to sound like a police whistle. After Rickard let out an even shriller signal, the three ran to join forces.

"How did it go?"

"Oh, fine. He . . . the fellow in the long robe . . . didn't know much about fighting. I used that 'Japanese hold' on him, and he went right down."

"Well, weren't there others who attacked you?"

"No. Evidently their rule was 'one against one.' For that matter, I suspect that they were pretty tired. Who knows how many miles they have to walk each day. Here's your cap. Did you have to look a long time for Pelle?"

"Oh, it took a while, of course. Finally, he heard me shouting and came running like a rabbit."

"Were you frightened, Pelle?"

"Just a little. . . . I just didn't like those children."

Jon and Rickard looked at Pelle tenderly as he stood there with his stool. They felt a real responsibility for him, realizing what he had had to experience thanks to their interference.

Rickard put down the bundle of clothing.

Jon said, "I'm absolutely starving. Rickard, don't you have *something* in your pockets?"

Rickard groped inside his baggy pants.

Since he had come to live with Per-Anders on Kalv Island, many things had changed in the life of "Svensson's boy." The most meaningful of all was that he no longer had to go hungry. The art of fine cooking was not among those mastered by the lonely old man, but there was always something in the cottage to chew on. There were apples—virtually an unknown luxury among the slum dwellers in Soltuna—in abundance. There were eggs, and there were potatoes in the cellar. From Uddesund on the mainland came rich milk. And if the fruits of the earth were to run low, which they never had to date, you could count on the fish in the lake.

What this meant to the boy from Quarry Road, who had been more or less hungry since the moment of his birth, was something no one but Rickard himself could know. The knowledge that he could stuff himself at will was ever present—it was there when he wakened and when he fell asleep, when he was cold and when he was hot. It was even there in his subconscious mind as he slept deeply on the little trundle bed in Per-Anders' scrubbed kitchen.

Jon sensed a bit of this. He alone knew his friend's one eccentricity.

Rickard always had a sack of food with him. He never overate. It was as if at the end of every meal he subconsciously saved the last bites as insurance against hard times, and the provisions that he carried in his shirt and pants pockets were, for the most part, untouched when he returned home. But they were there. He saw to it that he was never without some provisions.

At times they came in handy—such as right now.

From the deep interior of his clothing, Rickard took out a little paper bag containing zweiback, three eggs, and a number of newspaper-wrapped packages containing fried pork slices.

"Just as I thought! That devil of a herder boy crushed the zweiback. Oh, well, there they are in any case, and they won't taste any worse for being broken."

"Great," Jon said. "I'm as hungry as a bear. Blueberries don't stick to your insides very well, do they, Pelle?"

Eagerly, the child hopped up and down. Already he and Jon had removed their shoes and socks and had tried the temperature of the water with their toes.

"Let's have a swim first!" Rickard suggested. "The food won't run away!"

With care he laid out the provisions on a flat stone. Jon was happy once he had been informed that the eggs were hard-boiled. They could have turned out to be raw. Rickard was not very fussy. But of course they would have been difficult to carry that way.

The air had softened a bit, and it was still as warm as it had been in the middle of the day. Mist crept over the summery green slopes where the sun still shone, and there was no breeze to carry it away. All was completely still.

They took off their clothes, letting them fly in all directions to land on the coarse shore grass.

With Pelle between them, Jon and Rickard rushed into the water amid wild splashing.

Pelle let out an ear-splitting yell, but at last he had forgotten the stool. It remained standing on the flat stone where the food was, looking, for once, merely like a piece of furniture.

Above the boy's head, Rickard's and Jon's eyes met in almost fatherlike tenderness. Jon seemed ready to say something, but Rickard understood the words by mental telepathy: "Careful!" It was Pelle's first experience in the cold water, and he might have been frightened.

The surface of the water lay dark in the dull green

shadows of the alder shrubs. Clouds of insects swarmed in the foliage. Water spiders fled among the thin yellowish reeds.

From here you could see Kalv Island. It lay on the other side of the lake, looking for all the world like a camel with two humps.

"Smoke is coming out of the chimney there at home," Rickard said. All three stood still observing the smoke.

"Do you live there?" Pelle asked.

"Yes," Rickard replied. "I live there. Per-Anders must be cooking potatoes, I guess—or maybe perch. He caught a small perch yesterday."

The tone of his voice betrayed great pride.

Pelle looked up at him with wonder in his eyes. Rickard's head seemed uncommonly large now that his lanky, muscular frame was free of clothing. His hands, too, seemed huge. Meanwhile, Rickard glanced back at the "table" on shore to be sure that nothing threatened the food.

With a surprising lack of opposition, Pelle let them lead him to deeper water, where they could demonstrate swimming strokes to him.

"If you live near water, you have to be able to swim!" Jon declared.

Pelle shivered at first when the cold water reached above his navel.

"Don't keep your mouth open so wide," Jon advised. "You could get flies in your stomach!"

Giggling, Pelle took a step forward into deeper water.

"I think he's pretty brave," Rickard said, "when you consider that he's never been in the lake before!"

"It's not cold any more!" Pelle shrieked. "It's not cold any more!"

Some swallows took flight in formation across the bay. They, too, had their young to teach.

The adventure in the woods was not mentioned until they sat down by the flat stone at last and began to shell their eggs.

Then Jon said, "What a shame those herders were so surly that you had to fight with them! We should have been able to talk to them instead."

Rickard replied, "They spoke the language they've been forced to learn, I guess."

Jon was silent. Nothing more was said about the subject.

9

A Promise to Jon

THE cold September nights caused the mists to sweep across Vidar Lake's golden shore. In October the first big frost came.

Early in November the first snowflakes fell. Mother Nature was preparing herself for the long winter.

No doubt Jon had expected that he and Rickard would be even closer during this school year, their second at the Soltuna Consolidated Latin School, because they had shared so much during the summer vacation.

As had been decided upon at the District Council headquarters, the biology teacher, Mr. Ryd, had bicycled down to Sand Cape, taken the boys, and escorted them to the deserted moor up in the pine woods where *Pyrola umbellata* was growing. The blossoms at the top of the brittle stalks, both white and rose, bent toward the earth. It seemed unbelievable that something so fragile and beautiful could take root on the brownish hillocks.

The teacher, using a small pointed spade, dug up several choice specimens himself, wrapped the stalks in moss dampened in a nearby tarn, and supervised with caution the placing of them in Jon's collecting tin.

The teacher's deliberate movements and his erudite language turned the collecting of the plants into almost a religious ceremony. He gave the boys good advice, telling them, for example, to paint blue blossoms with saltpeter before pressing them so that they would hold their color.

Questioning them as to what had happened to Pelle and Alfrida, he was delighted to find that Pelle was under the protection of the doctor and his wife, though living with Alfrida.

To be sure, Jon and Rickard exchanged humorous glances behind the teacher's back that day, and later Rickard successfully mimicked the teacher's choice of words and prim tone of voice when they were alone in their hideaway beneath the veranda floor.

This always took place, however, in a spirit of amiable indulgence. There was something beneath the teacher's proper exterior for which the boys felt a great warmth. It had to do with his fairness, his sensitivity and goodness toward people, animals, and plants.

As for the teacher's correctness, the boys regarded it as a character trait. They knew well that he would never force himself on another person, no matter how young and insignificant.

The last weeks of the summer vacation slipped away. Like wild strawberries strung on a straw, they were soon consumed. The sweet almond blossoms had disappeared, and *Pyrola umbellata* was concealed between the pages of the herbarium book.

Jon felt that it was like peering through a long tube whenever he recalled the summer. With each passing day, the tube grew longer and longer, and the opening at the other end, where he could still see Sand Cape, the woods, and Vidar Lake, grew smaller and smaller.

His mental pictures of Pelle and Rickard diminished, too. This was not strange in the case of Pelle because Jon never saw him during the school year. It was a little more peculiar that he and Rickard, who had been in on so many things together and had always gotten along so well, were drifting apart. It made Jon depressed and confused.

More and more Rickard kept to himself in class. In the mornings he came less and less frequently to the doctor's home to pick up Jon after he had hopped off the Uddesund wagon at the public square. Once the day's classes were over, he disappeared on his own secret missions.

One afternoon, as Jon and his father drove along Quarry Road in the doctor's gig, pulled by the shiny, freshly groomed Figaro, Jon caught sight of Rickard.

He was standing there, hanging around the neighborhood of his old home, just like dozens of other youths and men the doctor and Jon had already seen in the courtyard entrances and outside the cafés in the course of their drive. Although he was only a boy, he looked just like them—like one of the unemployed.

"Shall we stop?" the doctor asked his son. "Do you want to talk to him?"

Jon realized that Father was leaving the decision up to him because he himself was uncertain—because he realized that the course of the boys' friendship had taken a new and strange turn.

"No, no I don't believe so," Jon said hastily. "I imagine he wants to be left alone."

They waved their hands in greeting as they rode by, and Rickard returned it in kind. But he didn't once alter his listless stance or the expression on his face.

"It's a terrible winter for the workers," Father said thoughtfully. "First there was the little strike early in the year, with some violence, especially at the quarry. Then the owners resorted to a lockout. That's an English term, actually, Jon, and it means that the owners close the place of employment and won't let the workers in. The owners, the employers, shut out the workers, and the factories close down."

"Then aren't the workers paid?"

"No, naturally not—not before the lockout is broken and they begin to cut stone again. The owners come through a work stoppage in pretty good shape. They have money in reserve. But the workers have nothing more than what they earn per day. They'll have to make the best of a bad situation and stop striking and using violence and continue as before."

"Was that why there was the big strike last summer?"

Jon had heard his father discuss the big strike before. Rickard also had told him about it, disjointedly and gloomily, as they were hanging Per-Anders' nets up to dry.

It had been most difficult for the working classes in the

cities since transportation and communications had been disrupted. In the villages the workers' socialist party had mounted huge signs: "FARMERS! PROVIDE THE CITIES WITH YOUR PRODUCTS. THINK OF OUR STARVING CHILDREN!"

Mother had climbed into the rowboat, and Jon had rowed her over to Per-Anders' cottage. She had wanted to find out for herself from Rickard how his little brothers and sisters were getting along in Soltuna. Later, she sent Soren to Quarry Road in the gig, which she loaded with flour, sugar, and butter.

Jon was not allowed to ride along. Fearfully, Mother talked about the assaults and disturbances and riots.

Father declared that the discontent of the workers and the earlier lockouts had led to the big strike.

"But, Father, who won out in the end?" Jon now asked. "Someone must have been the winner after all the riots."

Using his whip, Father pointed at the street corner they were just passing, where there was a beer parlor. Outside, groups of men, coatless and bareheaded in spite of the frosty air, crowded together. Their thin, worn jackets seemed to have collected all the reeking grayness of the quarry dust.

"Well, as you can see, they were not the winners! Unemployment is just as bad—in fact, even worse—than before. They had no savings to fall back on; they couldn't afford to hold out. It's just as it was in the past—the granite out at the quarry is coarse and hard to work with. They can't get out enough blocks fast enough for the cutters. The cutters go to the quarry and wait for days before getting a block suitable for cutting. While waiting, they are unemployed and earn nothing."

"But, Father, that just isn't right, is it? They can't help it if—well, they *want* to work!"

Jon was excited. Somewhere in all this, though the whys and wherefores eluded him, was the secret behind Rickard's hanging around his old home instead of doing his homework in Per-Anders' kitchen or helping him draw up the nets.

"Yes, you could say that. The workers didn't win out in the big strike. But, then, you can't say that the employers have been exploiting their defeat. It is perfectly clear to them that another such strike, if it includes all the workers in Sweden—or, at least, most of them—could be a defeat for them, too, and perhaps a national disaster."

"So, then, do you believe the workers at the quarry and other places have won something with their big strike in spite of it all?"

"Yes, I believe that for the first time they feel that they can accomplish things if they want to and if they stick together."

"Father, I want everyone to have the chance to work. Everybody! Rickard . . ."

"You're right about that. That should be the right of every human being. What were you about to say about Rickard?"

Figaro had shied away from a huge black and red poster that was flapping from a fence. Father applied the whip gently. They were on the way home.

"Well, as you probably know, Father, he's a socialist. He maintains that the next time the workers are going to set in motion an even bigger strike, a general strike!"

Jon looked up at his father, who had pulled his fur hat

down over his ears. His short black beard stuck out over his collar.

"Yes, I've heard about their plans for a general strike. They originate with the young socialists. They really haven't thought the matter through sufficiently. You see, they want everyone who has a job to stop working, or be forced by their co-workers to do so, until they get the wages they want . . ."

"Yes, but what if they can't achieve their rights any other way?"

"Gas, electricity, water, the cleaning industries, everything would stop functioning. Imagine, Jon, what the results of that would be! Everyone would be cold; contagious diseases would spread; the hospitals would collapse. In the country no one would care for the animals; the cows and horses would not get fed. There would be no crops. And I would have to take care of Figaro myself and close my reception room!"

Jon sat in silence. He decided he would have to speak to Rickard about this. He would . . . yes, he would.

"I'm sure Rickard hasn't thought of all these things. But I guess that's not so strange, is it, Father?"

"No, it's not strange, really. He sees and experiences so much more than you, Jon—misery and poverty, hopelessness. He has seen his father take to drink. Well, you know what it's like in the world."

Jon nodded. He knew a good bit, but far from enough.

"And," Father continued, "you know his older brothers are thieves and robbers. He's the only one to have come through all right. He has taken care of himself, but he's been lucky, too. Tell me, does he often go home to Quarry Road these days?"

"Much more often now, since the strike. I think that's very good of him. He doesn't want to *desert* them, you see, Father."

The black beard pointed upward. Jon noticed its silhouette against a gas lamp that had just been lighted.

"That's good," Father remarked. "He's a fine boy—and a very gifted one. He thinks for himself. There are many shameful conditions in society today. Sometimes it's as if we're stuck in a mire—that we're getting nowhere in combatting ignorance and poverty and dirt. But you, Jon, you and Rickard have to learn and teach others. You'll have to be helpful and not think merely of yourselves."

Gropingly, Jon said, "Sometimes when Rickard stays

home overnight, it's because he goes to protest meetings—those of the young socialists and others. Sometime if I'd like to go, Father, may I go along with him?"

Turning the corner, they rode along the edge of the doctor's property. Figaro quickened his pace. The stall and the feed bag!

For a moment silence reigned between the doctor and his son. Jon had scarcely had time to reflect upon the matter, but he had a quick foreboding that much depended on what Father was going to say. Much was at stake. Would Father react favorably to his appeal?

Father said, "Naturally, you may go if you want to."

But as they slowly entered the driveway and caught sight of the brass planter with the white begonias in the drawing-room window, he added, "Just don't say anything to Mother. She would probably give permission . . . but she would be worried."

10

The House of the Heaps

THERE were to be many long days before Jon saw Rickard again. The next morning his desk was unoccupied; it was the same the following day. On Monday morning their class advisor asked if anyone knew what had happened to Rickard Svensson. Was he sick? Could someone go to his home and give him his homework?

The teacher had the school register—the matriculation book, as it was called—in front of him. The pupils in the class were listed in alphabetical order. There were columns for such information as the year of their birth, the year they had entered the school, their addresses, and their fathers' occupations.

Meditatively, the teacher studied the column having to do with occupations, which included managing director, bookkeeper, school principal, wholesaler, district doctor, pharmacist.

Rickard Svensson's father was a quarry worker. Finding

this manual occupation listed in the Soltuna Consolidated Latin School's book was very uncommon—actually, unique.

The class advisor had let his eyes fall more than once on that unusual entry. Now he turned to Jon. Often he had seen the two boys together in the corridors and out on the schoolyard.

"Jon, can you find out anything about what has happened to Rickard?"

The teacher looked rather forbiddingly over his gold-rimmed glasses with their half lenses.

There was no way of his knowing what kind of home Rickard actually came from. He thought fleetingly of truancy.

Jon replied briefly but politely, "Yes, sir."

When school was over that day, he walked out to Quarry Road.

On the curb outside the tenements where "Svensson's boy" lived sat a couple of small children dressed in striped pinafores and knitted sweaters. Melted snow rushed along the gutter, for the first storm had quickly turned to grayish slush. One of the youngsters had a tin can and a rusty spoon, which she used as a scoop. To Jon's horror, the child suddenly put the tin can to her mouth and drank.

"Hey," Jon said. "You have no business drinking that water. It could be dangerous. Thousands of bacteria!"

The children stared at him. After a few moments' thought, the larger child once again filled the spoon with water. This time she offered it to the other, who swallowed it without blinking an eye but with a sidelong glance directed at Jon. His heart sank. He looked up at the high grayish-yellow exteriors of the buildings. Somewhere in one of the many apartments lived the Svensson family. Actually, these might be some of Rickard's brothers and sisters.

Jon peered inside the dark courtyard entrance. He felt that he was being observed by many eyes from on high, from the cellar casements, and from the other long rows of gloomy windows.

It was hardly possible that Rickard was here since nowadays his home was with Per-Anders on Kalv Island.

If he had become ill, he would be out there in bed.

Once more Jon cautioned the children, "Don't touch that dirty water!" Then he quickly walked back into the main part of town—much more quickly than he had come.

He felt cowardly and disconcerted and wondered what he would say to the teacher the next day.

The afternoon was clammy and nasty. Jon's thoughts were disorganized and slushy. They were like the flow of snow water in the gutter. It wasn't only the matter of Rickard. Jon was actually quite tired.

He had been awakened several times during the night. The telephone bell had jingled in his parents' bedroom, and Jon had heard his father's tired muffled voice, asking the usual questions: "Have you taken his temperature?"

Often as not the answer to that one was that there was not a thermometer in the house. Father would continue.

"Does he have chills? Is he perspiring? Do the pains move or does it just ache continuously in one place? Is the area tender when you touch it?"

The latter question always had to be repeated. It was impossible to ascertain clear facts. There were long pauses while the sick person and the remaining members of the family held a conference.

For the most part, no information at all was available, because the person calling was at the nearest telephone to home which might have been a mile or more away from the patient.

At times the conversations would end with simple advice.

"Don't give him anything to eat. No, not even water. Tomorrow morning try a cup of weak tea and a piece of toast without butter." Or, "Take a pinch of salt in a glass of water. Yes, call again tomorrow morning. My office will be open at seven."

Still more often the result was something else.

"All right, I'll come. I'll be there in half an hour. Number 78? Just beyond the commons. All right. See to it that the gate is open."

Between each sentence Jon longed to sink back into the beautiful realm of unconsciousness.

Thank heaven, Yan was now sleeping by himself in a tiny alcove, which had once been a clothes closet. It used to be that the ringing of the telephone would waken him, whereupon he would start to scream at the top of his lungs.

In the night Father had been summoned out on one sick call at two o'clock. The clock in the drawing room had struck just as he hung up the receiver—a brittle, silvery sound.

One additional call must have come, probably early in the morning and undoubtedly from far away, because when Jon left for school at seven, Father hadn't yet returned. The reception room was filled with patients, mostly workers from Soltuna, who had begun to bombard the nurse with questions, worried that they might not get to work on time that morning.

When Jon came home for lunch, Father was resting. The entire household walked around on tiptoe, hushing one another so that the doctor could have a little peace and quiet. When Figaro neighed from the yard, Soren was nearly held personally to blame.

Jon hoped that everything would have straightened itself out again in the afternoon. He had a long, boring arithmetic assignment that he had to get going on. And geography—the Balkan States . . .

Mother was sitting in a bishop's chair at a little drop-leaf table, preparing Father's bills to the residents of Soltuna when he came back from Quarry Road. The state paid a part of the workers' fees. Many things had to be filled in—names, numbers, the nature of the illnesses, and a whole lot besides. Piles of blank bills lay before her. There were additional blank pads on the windowsill. Mother also had Father's notes at hand, together with a rubber stamp with his name and a purple ink pad.

Naturally, Father himself didn't have the time to sign these hundreds of papers.

Mother was wearing a blouse with a white collar and a striped tie. Her hair was pulled up tightly into an enormous bun that looked like a crow's nest.

She put down her pen when she saw Jon in the doorway.

"Oh, Jon, I'm so glad you're here. I had begun to worry. Did you finish late at school today?"

Jon put his brown canvas schoolbag on the serving table at the door. Then he walked over to Mother and put his cheek against hers, rubbing it for a quick moment. Right away he knew that something had happened because Mother was not her usual smiling self, and she didn't bother to wait for an answer to her question.

"Something so dreadful has happened, Jon. I imagine you heard that Father had to go out early this morning as the result of a call, didn't you?"

"Yes . . ."

There was just time enough for one question. "Who . . . ?"

"It's Rickard's father, Jon. Such a terrible shame for them, the whole family. These dreadful strikes—all the hatred. . . . Oh, yes, Mari, that will be fine!"

Mari had come in with a tray holding Jon's cup of hot chocolate and a bread basket with rolls and pastries. On a corner of the dining table, she spread a small white cloth.

As though anxious not to disturb them, she looked neither at Mother nor Jon. Mother nodded.

"Thank you, Mari," she said absent-mindedly, adding quickly, "The butter pastries at lunch were delicious— even better than last time."

Jon also thanked her, and Mari disappeared through the door to the serving pantry, carrying her empty tray.

The cup of hot chocolate was steaming. Jon remained standing by Mother's chair.

"It was some time before Father could piece the whole story together. Svensson hadn't came home to Quarry Road for several days, and it was to a hut belonging to one of the woodcutters for the Vidinge property that Father was summoned this morning about four o'clock. He got there too late. The man had a gangrenous leg, and the poisoning had spread. Father was terribly upset, you see, because the whole thing needn't have happened!"

"But Rickard's father works at the quarry, doesn't he? He doesn't work in the woods."

"No, of course not. Oh, Jon, I just don't understand how people can make such a mess of things for one another!"

Though Mother put her hands up to her eyes, Jon knew that she wouldn't shed any tears. Only small children like Yan cried.

He sat on the floor beside the claw-footed leg of the drop-leaf table. Near him was a woolen rug woven in every color of the rainbow. With his finger Jon followed one of the complicated patterns.

"Is he dead?"

"He died just as they got him to the hospital—while they were carrying him up the steps."

"Was Rickard there?"

"Yes, the boy was along. His was that last call Father got this morning. He was calling from the phone at Fishing Square. You know, Jon, that the quarry workers began one of their so-called 'wildcat strikes' a week ago. They were striking for higher wages, but the main issue was the quarry blocks. If the quarry can't bring up enough stone blocks from the pit, the workers who cut the stone are technically unemployed, and they are forced to go out there and wait without being paid.

"It's just too ridiculous!

"The company management, the owners and those responsible for the quarrying, want to pay only for the actual work done. So you see that the cutters can be without work for days at a time when they are quarrying in a difficult area of the mountain and can't get blocks out very quickly. The cutters took part in the big strike last summer, Jon, as you know, and lost what little they had. And now this new strike on top of it!

"Well, it seemed that they were expecting blocks suitable for cutting out at the quarry, but the cutters refused to touch them before getting an agreement guaranteeing them a certain hourly wage regardless of whether there was work to do or not. Just by coincidence the rumor got around that the company would pay double time to anyone willing to go back to work . . ."

"You mean willing to break the strike, don't you, Mother? To be a strikebreaker?"

Jon knew how dangerous such a move could be. Not sticking together with your co-workers but following the wishes of the employers—all this could make the strike meaningless.

"Exactly. But you have to understand what an enormous temptation it is for many of them to get back to work. The workers are starving. Most of them have families to support. Rickard has three or four younger brothers and sisters at home, hasn't he?"

Jon's mouth was half open. His eyes and hair were a dark contrast to his pale face. His summer tan had vanished, so that there was only a trace of color left.

"And then"—Mother suddenly looked Jon straight in the eye, and he knew that she was going to say something that was usually not discussed in the presence of children, but Jon was usually told the whole truth, and that was the most important of all—"I guess Rickard's father didn't really have much concern for his family, but more for whiskey."

"I know," was Jon's quick reply.

"There are people who just can't get along without whiskey. Their environment—well, I guess they think there's nothing else to life. And they get cold—it's so bitter cold out at the quarry."

"I know!"

Mother nodded.

"Anyway, that was the way it was. Svensson and a couple of like-minded workers took off for the quarry and began to cut some stone blocks. They hoped, of course, that they could keep it a secret and that none of their co-workers would go out there in the bitter weather—maybe, even, that others would follow their example and put a gradual end to the strike.

"But instead they were discovered. The other workers, determined to get revenge against the strikebreakers, marched out there in full force. There was a riot, and mounted police were called. A couple of the strikebreakers were seriously injured, and worst of all was Rickard's father."

Mother looked at the hot chocolate that had stopped steaming. But it was as if she didn't see it—or, at least, didn't care a thing about it.

"His leg was injured right below the knee—a deep wound that was bleeding profusely. He tried to get back into the town after tying up his leg, but on the way he saw some of his striking co-workers—saw them at a distance across the flatlands—and realized he was trapped. He fled up into the woods."

Mother picked up the rubber stamp and pressed it to

the ink pad. Then she pressed it against the bill on the top of the pile.

"How he could ever get as far up in the Vidinge woods as he did, especially with that deep a wound, Father says he can't understand. But it seems that eventually Rickard's father was found by one of the woodcutters, who took him to his hut. There he was left alone because the woodcutter had just finished his work there and had cut all the trees marked for cutting in that part of the woods."

Mother put down the rubber stamp. She couldn't even concentrate on a simple job like this. Cross-legged, Jon was sitting on the rug. His eyes never left her face. He watched every change in her expression.

"In any event, the woodcutter was a good samaritan who wouldn't leave a fellow man in distress. He didn't know how to dress the wound, but when he returned home to his village, he went past the home of Ottilia of Brannehult. The woman is a sort of quack doctor, you remember, Jon, the one about whom Alfrida talked last summer."

Jon remembered. Father had shaken his head in disbelief when he heard about certain of the salves, herb compotes, and other remedies Ottilia used. Alfrida herself had gone to Ottilia for help with the gout, she had said, and when Father advised her to go to a real doctor instead, she merely pursed her lips, looked all-knowing, and said, "Ottilia of Brannehult isn't stupid, not at all. She knows a little of this and that, which she learned long ago from her mother!"

"Did Ottilia go to see Rickard's father?"

"Yes, she went immediately. And you can't imagine what she did! It could send you out of your mind just thinking about it! How can people in our times be so ignorant! She's a woman of some experience, and she knew that there was danger of blood poisoning and gangrene, so she applied her usual remedy, which is potato alcohol and salt! And that's what she treated Svensson's leg with!"

Jon was wide-eyed.

"But, Mother, you can't mean that she . . ."

"Yes. She has an old booklet that she inherited from her mother, and that's where she has learned all these atrocities. Father had heard of this ancient cure—he actually ran into it some time ago in one of the out-of-the-way places, but he was unaware that faith in it was still prevalent in this area. In town here, people no longer go to quacks and sorcerers.

"The remedy consists of mixing ground salt with potato alcohol and letting it stand for half an hour. Then the patient is given a spoonful of it, and the wound, head or stomach or wherever, is rinsed with a piece of linen dipped in the mixture. Ottilia had done all this conscientiously."

"And did he still get blood poisoning?"

"Of course. The poor man! Ottilia visited him every single day, but she's not a very antiseptic person. Her pig stays inside the cottage with her when it's cold, as you know, Jon! She's proud of her skills, and she was happy to have a chance to practice them. She took food to

Svensson, too. The woodcutter felt that he had arranged matters beautifully for his guest, and nothing was heard from him again."

Mother began to stamp the bills once more, first to the pad, then to the blanks. The pile before her grew.

"Rickard's father would probably have died there in the hut in the woods if Ottilia hadn't come down to the village, talking and bragging about how well she was caring for her patient. The Uddesund farmer got wind of the story, and since he knew that Rickard's father had disappeared after the riot on the road to the quarry, he came to his own conclusions. He and Rickard went up there late yesterday evening. There are no roads or paths in that area of the woods, and they had a difficult time finding the hut in the dark. It's hard to believe that Rickard could manage to make his way right from the deep woods to the telephone at Fishing Square. It must have been a good many miles, Jon. And then, as it turned out, it was too late. . . . Father"—Mother's voice sank to a whisper—"was so concerned. He had found the booklet about 'Alcohol and Salt, a remedy' in the hut. 'Just as infallible for wounds as for a plague of worms' was what it said. Ignorance—rank ignorance, all of it."

Jon sat in silence. He was thinking of Rickard, who had said the same thing, but in a situation far different from Father's.

"It's because of ignorance that people are held down. They let children become herders instead of teaching them to read, and they continue to be held down!"

Jon arose stiff-legged, as if from the cold, and walked

over to his barely warm chocolate. There was a scum on it. Jon detested the scum. Using his spoon, he removed it cautiously so as not to leave any of it floating in the cup. But his action was mechanical, from force of habit. He could have swallowed the scum at this point without even noticing.

It was quiet in the room. From the cellar came a rhythmic dunk, dunk, dunk, dunk. Mari was at the mangle, ironing. All around her, Jon knew, were piles of sheets, pillowcases, and towels. He could almost sense the refreshing odor of clean linens, even upstairs. Once again he recalled something Rickard had said. It hadn't sounded nasty or envious when he had said it—more reflective, half apologetic.

"It seems to me that the doctor's house is full of piles of things. I used to say to myself, 'I am going over and see Jon who lives in the house with the heaps!' The first time I came here there were piles of warm rolls in a towel-covered basket on the kitchen table. And your little brother's diapers lay in a pile by the window. Things are piled up at the mangle, and, well, even Figaro's horse blankets are piled up in the stall. And your mother sits and nods behind piles of your father's newspapers or clothing. Sometimes it's only piles of bills she's working with, but everything turns out to be in a pile."

Rickard had said that long ago, while they were still in elementary school. Jon wondered if he would still notice it.

Stirring his chocolate absent-mindedly, he took a bite of one of the rolls. It seemed almost dry in his mouth, although it was really fresh. He knew that certain ideas awaited him, things that he would have to puzzle out whether he wanted to or not—about the desolateness of the area, about Rickard's dying father—thoughts of the future, and what it would be like when he saw Rickard again.

Mother went on with her stamping. One pile grew; the other diminished. Jon sat quietly at the corner of the table with the white cloth.

His mother talked, half to herself.

"Is it really true that you experience everything so early? I just don't remember. . . . It's hard for a grown-up to know what to say, how to act when he sees a close friend after a tragedy. I wonder how the boys will work this out between themselves? But I'll never know, of course. And nobody can help them."

11

You Have to Find Out

RICKARD didn't return to school for a whole week. Father informed Jon that he had gotten a severe cold during the fateful night and that, after his father's death, he had ridden out with the Uddesund farmer to Kalv Island.

"It's warmer and more comfortable there," Father explained.

But early one morning the following week, when Jon came half running down the garden path on the way to school, he saw a shadowy form moving just beyond the gate.

It was a well-known figure. Suddenly Jon came to life.

"Hi, there," the shadowy figure said.

"Hi, yourself," Jon responded.

It was still dark on this cold, frosty morning. The boys walked down the street toward the public square, side by side.

As they passed the circle of light beneath a gas lamp,

Jon, watching their shadows reaching far out onto the cobblestones of the street, noticed that Rickard's was a good bit longer than his own. Rickard was wearing the old jacket that he had acquired in the used-clothing shop on Fishing Square. There was no change in his outward appearance except for the black crepe band around one arm. Jon looked sideways at the armband.

Both of the boys had thought about, and pretty much knew, what they ought to say to one another. But neither could put his thoughts into words.

Their boots creaked. The snow on the paving stones crunched under the soles of their boots. Jon pretended momentarily to be interested in the shop windows, but when one turned out to be women's fashions and the other a butcher shop with a row of half sides of pork, he gave up.

Rickard broke the silence.

"How has it been going at school?"

The question had a faraway quality to it, as if Rickard himself had been on a long journey.

"Oh, nothing new. Nothing special at all. Well, we do have a new substitute in math and the class has been really rude to him."

Jon said "the class," not "we." He and Rickard never behaved in a rude way. They couldn't even explain why themselves.

Jon continued to tell stories of what the "worst" boys in the class had come up with. Nothing about his account was earth-shaking or even amusing, but Rickard laughed abruptly, loudly, and harshly.

The corners of Jon's mouth began to turn upward. It

meant a lot—Rickard's laughter—and Jon realized this at once. Life was difficult for Rickard, but he *wanted* to have fun; he *wanted* to return to the classroom—and to Jon.

"Did the teacher ask about me? I have a written excuse from Per-Anders that I've been sick. . . . Oh, and how did it go with the high-jump meet for the first class? Was that little stiff fellow selected for the team?"

By the time Jon and Rickard crossed the large rectangular schoolyard, they were totally absorbed in one another. They looked like a couple of civil servants on the way to their posts. They were talking a mile a minute.

At the first recess, they walked back and forth across the

schoolyard, shoulder to shoulder. Rickard asked Jon if he had heard about all that had happened in connection with his father.

At the next recess, Jon asked Rickard how he could have made it from the hut in the big woods to the town in the darkness of night.

"It wasn't as difficult as you might have expected, because it happened to be a clear, starry night, and I could calculate from the Big Dipper. I knew that Soltuna was to the north. But it was cold, and I had a long way to go. Now and then I ran. The Uddesund farmer had said that time was of the utmost necessity. Actually, I knew that without his telling me . . ."

"I wish," Jon remarked, "I wish Father had wakened me and taken me along."

"Your father," Rickard said slowly, sounding for all the world as if he were making an important pronouncement, "your father was, well, he was just great. He managed to construct a stretcher out of bunk frames from the hut and some long willow branches. He and the Uddesund farmer carried it to a timber road and then onto the country road. He woke up some people in a house in the woods and borrowed a horse and carriage. And he rode in the carriage himself. The farmer and I rode in the gig, which Figaro pulled. Your father had left it at the estate's gate when we took off for the woods. My father . . ."

Jon wished he could have hit upon something nice to say about Rickard's father. He wanted to get across something about how different people are from one another, how unlike they are born, how their souls are just as different, the one from the other, as their faces and bodies!

But he could scarcely start a discussion with Rickard on the subject of souls here in front of the entrance to the school, especially not with the supervising teachers on tours of inspection of the garbage cans, where a gang of first-year students were up to some sort of mischief.

Instead, he asked, "How are you going to get along now? I mean, how will it be for your mother and your little brothers and sisters?"

Rickard turned his head aside. Several minutes elapsed before he regained control of his voice.

"Well, I guess they won't be any worse off. You remember what they said—the men at the auction in the district headquarters—don't you? As long as there's a man at the head of a family, the Public Assistance Commission won't give a penny in help. Now that my mother's a widow, I believe somehow that . . . that she'll be better off."

They were interrupted by the ringing of the school bell. Shivering with cold, they joined the group streaming toward the classroom. Rickard seemed to have a look of contentment on his thin face. A burden had fallen from him when he had been able to tell Jon what the doctor had accomplished during that difficult night.

As usual, Rickard had his lunch bag with him, ready to eat at school, as they walked down the steps after the morning classes.

"Are you going to ride home with the Uddesund farmer tonight, out to Per-Anders' cottage?"

Rickard shook his head.

"No, I think I'll stay in town."

"But you're going to keep on living with Per-Anders as before, aren't you?"

"Certainly. I'm just going to stay in Soltuna tonight, that's all."

Something in Rickard's tone of voice made Jon careful. They remained standing at the foot of a broad, winding stone stairway that led up to the assembly room. The side walls were decorated with a number of copper plaques portraying the monarchs of Sweden. Rickard turned his back on the stern profile of Gustav Vasa.

Not wishing to ask Rickard directly about his plans for the evening, Jon waited to see what his friend would say. Rickard looked to one side.

"There's going to be a protest meeting in the late afternoon outside the Community House. The young socialists are in back of it—for that matter, the meeting has been in the planning stages for quite a long time. I'm sure you've seen the posters all over town. Red and black . . ."

Jon recalled the unfastened poster that had frightened Figaro. It had been as red as fire. He nodded.

"At this point the protest meeting is more important than ever. Several of the older people are thinking of giving up and breaking the strike by going back to their jobs at the quarry. But the young socialists want to stop them. An agitator is coming to the meeting from headquarters in Stockholm."

Searchingly, Jon looked up at Rickard's face.

"Do you agree with the young socialists?" he asked. He

was recalling what Father had said about the needless injury of people. The young socialists had been back of the march out to the quarry the day Rickard's father had been forced to flee on his injured leg.

"I just don't know," Rickard said thoughtfully. "I was completely in agreement with them before. One of my brothers is a young socialist. People just can't sit around and wait endlessly. You have to *do* something *now*. And fight if it's necessary.

"But since it all happened—all that business out at the riot—I just don't know. That's why I want to go to the meeting and hear what they have to say. You have to find out for yourself. If the workers are in the right—and they are—then we have to . . ."

Rickard stopped talking. A couple of teachers were coming down the steps.

Jon said, "I'm coming along."

"To the meeting?"

"Yes. I want to hear, too—and see how it all goes."

Rickard had been standing a step higher than Jon. At this point he stepped down. He lowered his voice.

"But it might be dangerous."

"I know that."

"Jon, the police don't have any use for the young socialists. The school doesn't, either. If anyone were to see us, or if we were to become involved . . . well, I don't want you to . . ."

A few moments before there had been something about the expression on Rickard's face that Jon didn't exactly like—something having to do with the fact that there were things that Jon didn't understand, couldn't understand. But in that split second, all this had disappeared. Rickard's dark gray eyes looked straight at Jon's. What he had intended to convey was obvious. He didn't want to put Jon in any danger.

Seeing his chance, Jon jumped in.

"I get it. You don't want me to hear . . . and see what's going on, huh! That's what you mean, isn't it?"

Rickard stood there quietly. He bit his lips, but his serious face lighted up in a surprising manner.

"That was cleverly put, Jon. Of course, you're right. And you can bet I won't try to stop you. I want you along, want to hear what you think. If we don't get a chance to talk after gym, why don't we make some plans right on the spot. We'll meet at four, say at . . . well, at the little bridge in the city park."

"Four o'clock," Jon confirmed. "I'll see you."

Conspiratorially, they winked at one another. Jon rushed out the school gate.

Rickard wandered down the entrance hall toward a smaller stairway that led to the basement. There was a little kitchen there, supervised by the janitor, and a room with a long table and benches where pupils who lived far from school could eat their package lunches.

Dust, chalk, wool, leather, rank cleaning fluids—all the special smells of the school hit Rickard's nostrils. He seemed to be enjoying the sensation. These gray white walls and the worn, scraped benches with the many drawings and scribblings gave him a feeling of warmth, of belonging, of a promise for the future. Because it had been many hours since he had eaten his morning meal on Kalv Island, he was terribly hungry. Soon he would be full. In some inexplicable way, Jon stood very much in the picture Rickard had of his future. Come to think of it, he was very much behind the whole thing.

12

The Protest Meeting

THE Community House was some distance from the doctor's home, on the other side of the city park, quite near the commons.

During the summer the workers' meetings had been held out of doors in the open fields. They had served as excursion points for the workers' families, who had appeared with picnic baskets, camped out in the open, and listened to brass bands and popular orators. Mr. Palm, at that time a veteran labor agitator, had attracted huge crowds.

As winter approached, however, the crowds thinned out. The spirit of the community or family party had disappeared. An old grain store had been renamed the Community House. It had neither central heating nor other comforts, but at least it was a shield against wind and weather. To a large extent, the meetings had been held inside.

Today, since there was to be a demonstration and parade, the broken-down shack was deemed too limited in space. The young socialists wanted to attract attention. They wanted to be seen and, even more important, to be heard.

Meeting at the little rolling bridge that crossed Tuna River, the boys could hear the brass sextet even from that distance. Along the narrow street, which ended at the commons, they saw no less than six uniformed police constables with spiked helmets, coats with shiny yellow buttons, and hanging swords. One of them had a much wider yellow band on his sleeve and his stand-up collar.

"That man," Rickard whispered, "is the commissioner."

At that moment a group of eight or ten young men passed them. The one in the lead carried a red banner fluttering in the wind, so huge that it seemed to occupy the space between the walls of the houses.

When the marchers heard the music of the brass band playing at the Community House, they joined in and began to sing at the tops of their lungs:

"Here among the workers young leaders take their part.
 Beneath their flaming banner, they give it soul and
     heart!"

The melody was lively and stirring. Jon and Rickard exchanged amused glances, and both began to laugh. The singing troops pushed the boys toward a street corner, but that didn't seem to matter. They hopped up on the curb and regarded the whole thing with amusement.

They started out again, this time a little behind the group. On the other side of the street, in the doorway of

a book and stationery store, a constable had taken his
position. He looked very authoritative, and Jon had the
impression that he was observing both of them attentively.

Jon's hand moved toward his school cap.

"Maybe we ought to remove our caps. They were the
cause of so much trouble before."

But Rickard shook his head.

"Here, I think, it will prove to be just the opposite.
It's just as well to let the policemen know that we're private school pupils. That will make them think we're
'proper people'!"

The tone of Rickard's voice was scornful, but Jon didn't

show any resentment. What he said was true, actually, even
if it was unjust—the children of "proper people" could also
be found in the public school.

By now they had caught sight of the barracks-like Community House. The autumn day had been clear and cloud-
less. Daylight had lingered longer than usual, but dusk
was beginning to fall. The gas lamps were lighted—perhaps unnecessarily, you might say, as you looked at the
vaulted greenish sky with one twinkling star rising above
the commons.

"Rickey," Jon said. "I think you'd better tell me what
I'm in for. What do they say? How do they act? Where do
they come from?"

Rickard knew at once what Jon was getting at with his
questions. He wanted them both to forget where they
had come from, forget the differences in their environment and training. It had to do with what Rickard and
Jon wanted to find out—not with the boy from the doctor's home and the boy from the slums.

During his short life, Rickard had heard many words
of envy, of hatred and threat. He was trying to forget
them for the moment. He wanted to live up to Jon's ex-
pectations. Jon was there for the purpose of learning
about things as they really were. He was certainly aware
that he wouldn't learn them at home, though the subjects might be touched upon now and then. Rickard
truly wanted to do his best. He thought for a while before replying.

"They demonstrate so that workers will have their lot
improved. Every speech is geared to that. Higher wages,

better living quarters, security—against being laid off wherever and whenever it's convenient to the owners. This is very important. They also want shorter working hours."

Jon nodded. He found it unthinkable that anyone could possibly disagree with these principles.

"And then," Rickard resumed, "there are lots of other things that aren't as they should be. They feel that all children should be given a chance to go to school and study and learn—all who want to and have the ability, that is. And then there's the business of the county rotation. You saw for yourself what that was about last summer—and they want it abolished."

"But everything you've mentioned is only right!" Jon said. "Do they really have to riot over those things?"

Rickard stuck his hands in his pockets. In the one was a hard-boiled egg, which he had in mind to eat in the evening. His lunch had been substantial, and he wasn't yet hungry. The janitor's wife, as usual, had offered him a huge bowl of oatmeal.

"No," he said, "there shouldn't be riots. Mr. Branting —you know who he is, the Labor Commissioner in the Parliament up in Stockholm—even says that all these things will come if we just stick together and don't give up. The people now have the right to vote—not the women, of course, but every man.

"And still," Rickard said as he fingered his egg, "it's quite different if you have to go hungry. If you haven't any place to live, you don't want to sit around and wait for an affirmative answer from the rich people!"

While the boys were thus lost in their thoughts, the crowds along the sides of the street had grown. Now they were overflowing into the street. Out here there was no paving; the street was rough and bumpy and crisscrossed by frozen wagon tracks.

Just before the street ended at the plaza in front of the Community House, there was a new cross street, wide and cobblestoned, with recently built houses of several stories on both sides. Jon realized that the nearby older buildings were condemned. They looked as if they were crouching and collapsing in the wake of the overwhelming new and encroaching modern ones.

The new buildings were impressive. Alabaster in color, they rose in a sort of polished majesty. On the ground floor were small shops for tobacconists, florists, candy dealers. Wide balconies with black wrought-iron railings were suspended loftily above the street from the highest floors. The entryways were "guarded" by stone statues with strange heads and even stranger feet. Their hands bore garlands that twined about complicatedly, covering the façades. The doors consisted of huge glass panes with mahogany frames. Inside were marble stairways, soft rugs, and often a smaller door behind which was the watchful eye of the doorman.

Rickard waved a hand at one of the new buildings. There were only five of them, but it was quite evident that this was the future fate of this part of the city, and of the commons as well.

"You can tell," he said, "that there's money in Soltuna. In just one of these buildings . . ."

He got no farther because at the same moment the boys passed the elegant quarter, they heard shrill police whistles from several directions. From the corner of the farthest of the new houses, a troop of mounted police was on the way.

"I'm sure the shop owners in the new buildings have sent for the mounted police," Rickard muttered in Jon's ear. "They're worried about their showcase windows. Last time a couple of them got broken."

They heard the snorts of the horses and the clip-clop of their hoofs. As they left the cobblestone street, the noises changed. The hoofs seemed to scrape against the frozen earth. The riders sat straight, motionless, and calm in their saddles. The bodies of the horses swayed rhythmically, almost in unison. They took up a good bit of room, and since the open square in front of the Community House had begun to be filled by demonstrators and an ever increasing group of curious onlookers from the nearby streets, things were fairly crowded.

Rickard grabbed Jon's hand. They felt a little silly, as if they were playing a game in elementary school, holding hands. Jon grinned sheepishly, somewhat embarrassed. Rickard said, "We don't want to get separated!"

Red and black banners floated high. They rose and fell above the heads of the crowd. Several women with long skirts and leaflets in their hands squeezed through the crowd. They made their way forcibly, handing out leaflets. Rickard got one stuffed into his hand. Jon read the title. He had never seen it before. It was called, "Storm Warning."

In front of the broken-down stairway of the Community House was a platform with a lectern that had been constructed of packing cartons. The wooden slats on the lectern had been covered by cloth in the colors of the Swedish flag. High up were red banners. As background for these hung white cloths resembling sheets. The legend on them, in red, said: "Down with the altar, the throne, the sword, and the moneybag."

The band was playing at full volume. Familiar melodies wafted above the heads of the crowd, out over the commons, over the shacks that had survived almost everything, over the newly constructed buildings, whose glittering windows seemed to blink in astonishment, if not fear.

"I just don't understand . . ." Rickard mumbled as his eyes searched the crowd. "I really don't get it . . ."

"The Internationale," battle hymn of the world-wide labor movement, echoed against the walls of the buildings. The frenzied blare of the trumpets could doubtless be heard all over Soltuna.

Never in his life had Jon found himself in a gathering like this. The music and the voices, gathering momentum with every second, carried him along with them. The mounted troops came so close to the boys that they could smell the horses.

Jon's hand, still in Rickard's, had grown damp. He made an attempt to free himself, but Rickard refused to relax his grip. A group of half-grown boys, probably from the public school, shoved them in the back, talking and swearing.

Jon looked up at Rickard, who stood on tiptoe. Around them the din rose and the crowd swelled.

Rickard came back down on his heels.

"Don't let go. We just can't get separated. I know what's going on now. Right behind the police horses is a troop of workers. I'm sure they're on their way to the quarry to go back to work. Why did they have to pick this time and place? Now I see why they have the mounted police out. Push your cap down, Jon!"

His warning came just in the nick of time. Jon received a terrible shove in the back from a large man, who had evidently been drinking, just as the call went forth. "Stop them! Stop the devils!" He pushed his way toward the platform.

The last few measures of "The Internationale" wafted out over the crowd. The ensuing silence was so unexpected that people seemed to quiet down at once. Through the calm came a monotonous and strangely chilling voice, in great contrast to the excitement of a few moments ago.

Jon noticed that someone had mounted the podium, but no matter how hard he strained, he couldn't hear what was being said.

Rickard said, "That's not the young socialists. That's the police commissioner speaking!"

They could only catch a few words. ". . . the law . . . insurgence . . ." Then: "Right of passage . . . the assembled . . . make room . . . if not . . . disperse . . ."

Sharp, clear vowels made certain words audible.

Rickard looked around as if he were planning something. They were right in the middle of the mob. The howling schoolboys nearby had grown quiet; they looked frightened.

The police commissioner left the lectern, which remained empty for a few moments. Then a troop of young socialists marched up with an enormous red banner, which cracked against the flagpole as it was hoisted up on the platform.

When the notes of a brief trumpet fanfare had died away, the words of command were spoken. A murmur rolled through the crowd. Someone shouted, "The police! They're going to charge!"

After that neither Jon nor Rickard could get their bearings or stop to evaluate the situation. Panic reigned. The crowds surged, screamed, and went off in all directions. The tumult heightened.

A series of pictures and sounds, all without continuity, passed before Jon's eyes and through his mind. Fear—complete, unreasoning—ruled him entirely—perhaps for the first time in his life. The leaflets floating through the air, the shining brass instruments, horses, monstrous in their enormity as they towered over the milling mob with quivering nostrils, the whites of their eyes gleaming . . .

And in the midst of these pictures, memories of bygone days, the front door at home, the pillars in the assembly hall, the first page of Selma Lagerlöf's *The Wonderful Adventures of Nils,* which they read at school in the mornings, the silver ribbon of Tuna River beneath the little bridge where they had met, he and Rickard, just a half hour ago . . .

A horse moved his head close to Rickard's ear, and Jon

was pushed by its massive hindquarters. He would have fallen had it not been for Rickard's uncompromising grip. Rickard held fast, pulling him, tugging him, refusing to give up. He had a goal, and untiringly he was pushing toward that goal like an animal, with shoulders and head bent. He wanted to make his way to the new street, clear to the farthest of the new buildings. He could see them gleaming with lights in the windows, towering above the tumult around the Community House, undisturbed in their shielding security.

Jon's ears were buzzing. He had lost his bearings entirely. A couple of times he was pushed so hard from both sides that he had to gasp for breath. But Rickard kept his sharp elbows akimbo, using them to aid his progress forward. He had been to these things before and was not overwhelmed, as Jon was, by the hasty switch from the expectant party mood to riot and utter panic.

The police were under orders to disperse the protest meeting and to protect the strike-breaking workers. Rickard knew that they would do their duty well and that even innocent bystanders such as himself and Jon were there at the risk of life and limb. He noticed the mounted police ready to charge. The newly constructed houses with all the glass panes must be protected.

Quickly, Rickard calculated where the crowd would be the worst. In Jon's befuddled condition, it seemed a whole eternity to him, but actually it was only a few minutes before they landed in a relatively safe place.

Behind them they heard the neighing of the police horses, women screaming, the noise of the platform being stormed. They didn't look back. Together with others who had managed to free themselves from the mob, they moved as quickly as possible up the wide new street.

The police had formed a cordon at the corner. Panting, those in flight halted. Jon had a pain in his chest, and his eyes seemed out of focus.

The police cordon separated in the middle of the street.

At that same moment, a shot was fired behind them. Something came flying through the air—a sizzling, burning object.

Sharp words of command penetrated the area between the walls of the buildings. The police cordon closed again.

It all happened so rapidly that those running away scarcely had time to halt. Some of them hit against sword sheaths and the broad backs of the police. Others stumbled and fell down.

Rickard and Jon were among those in the lead. One second before the cordon of police closed again, Rickard ducked down. His grip on Jon's hand was like a lock.

Jon was swept along. He felt the arm of a uniform graze his forehead and had no idea how they got through, but the next moment they were free, rushing wildly up the street. Someone behind them shouted, "Stop, you! Halt!"

In the florist's window, between the yellow and purple chrysanthemums, they could see the reflections of panic-stricken faces. The burning object landed on the other side of the street, setting fire to a wheelbarrow.

The boys ran.

Rickard glanced quickly over his shoulder. He saw two constables leave the police cordon. He calculated the distance to the entryway of the second building in the row. Would he and Jon have time to get there?

Jon also looked around.

He managed to say, "The police! Rickard, hadn't we better . . ."

Breathlessly, Rickard said, "We'll make it . . . quick . . . in here . . ."

They had gotten to the entrance. It looked uncompromisingly locked, but Rickard pressed a white button on the panel. There was an answering buzzer, and Rickard pushed Jon inside. Behind them the entrance door locked.

They were in an impressive entry hall. Above their

heads opened a small window in a massive door of mahogany. Fierce eyes beneath a tuft of gray hair inspected them.

A feminine voice said, "Who did you want?"

Jon leaned against the wall without understanding what was going on. He had bit his tongue. There was a salt taste in his mouth. How could Rickard have imagined that they could make a getaway here? Get away! Why? Actually, they had done nothing wrong.

By the time Rickard responded, he had taken a couple of deep breaths and straightened his school cap.

"Mr. Ryd, the teacher."

The doorman's wife wore glasses that glistened in the light from the ceiling chandelier.

"Three flights up, and to the right! Go ahead!"

Her tone of voice changed to one of welcome and protectiveness. A stairway with five steps led to a smaller hall with a double stairway. Just as Rickard and Jon turned there, they glimpsed two huge shadows behind the entrydoor panes.

From the landing at the second floor, they heard the voice of the doorman's wife again, this time sounding rather confused.

"Who did you want?"

13

The Teacher

"I KNEW that he lived here, you see," Rickard said on the stairway, by way of explanation. "I have been here before talking to him about my plants. Three hundred specimens. And it was fine. He . . . he's a great guy!"

Jon licked his lips. "But listen, why were we running down the street that way? What good did that do us? Now the police will believe that we really did something, won't they?"

Jon leaned breathlessly against the polished wooden handrail. His eyes were clouded, his face was white, and he had to fight to regain control of his breathing.

"Well, you saw for yourself," Rickard replied quickly. "Someone had begun to throw burning rags at the police and the horses. If we had stuck around, they would have arrested us, and we would have had to give our names and addresses. The police would almost surely have reported us to the school. And the headmaster! Jon, don't you realize that we can be expelled for no other reason than just being under suspicion?"

Bass voices blending with the shriller tones of the doorman's wife reached them from the stairway below. Jon turned halfway around. It looked as if he intended to stop fleeing and go down and make some explanation. Abiding by the law was in Jon's blood.

But Rickard put his hand on Jon's arm. Looking at him warmly, he managed to find the right words.

"Jon, I don't want you to think I am standing up for the ones who were shooting out there, or the ones throwing smoke bombs and opposing the police. They're crazy, and they're just making matters worse. But even if you were to get away with it—and you would because you're the doctor's son—it might be very bad for me. You *know* who I am!"

Jon's jaw didn't drop. Instead, he clenched his teeth. All of a sudden, it seemed to him as if he and Rickard had become one person. It was a marvelous feeling, and he wasn't alone. It hit both of them simultaneously.

"Quick," Jon whispered, keeping one eye on the stairs down below. "What shall we do?"

Rickard tossed his head lightly, certain of victory.

"Come on!"

They took the next stairway two steps at a time, quietly and as quickly as a couple of cats.

They stood outside a door with a shiny brass knob and a black glass nameplate.

Excited voices from the entrance now echoed against the domed roof. Perspiration dripped from Jon. His shirt was sticking fast to his back and under his arms. In sheer exhaustion he stared at the red walls, a curious contrast to the white marble of the stairs. Perhaps he was seeing everything in a state of shock.

Rickard rang the ivory doorbell at the side of the door. The ring seemed weak but audible inside.

Rickard looked up at the ceiling.

What if no one were home! What if no one opened the door!

There was the rattle of a chain being drawn to one side. Suddenly, the door was unlocked.

There stood a plump middle-aged woman with a blue dress and a white apron—the teacher's housekeeper.

Rickard recognized her immediately, and—what was more important—she recognized Rickard. She was quite accustomed to visits by schoolboys to leave or collect their herbariums. The exchange of specimens was a part of the second year course in biology.

Jon and Rickard removed their caps and held them against their chests.

"Could we please speak with the teacher?"

The housekeeper nodded genially.

"Step right in. The teacher didn't tell me he was expecting anyone, but come on in, both of you. What are your names?"

"Rickard Svensson."

"Jon Halvorsson."

She disappeared to announce them. Closing the outer door behind him, Jon nodded in relief.

"What in the world," he whispered anxiously, "what in the world are you going to say?"

"I think I'll ask to take my herbarium. He kept it to

show the other second year classes my *Pyrola umbellata,* you remember."

"Yes, boys. The teacher is in his workroom. Go right along in," the housekeeper said as she returned to the room.

The corners of the room inside were dark. On an oval table, covered with an embroidered felt cloth with long fringe, was a tall lamp with a yellow glass shade. This illuminated the bookcases all around the walls, Oriental rugs, leather chairs, and an enormous mahogany sofa with a pillared back. At the foot of the lamp was a familiar object: a scroll of red fabric, rolled up like a sausage.

The teacher stood over near one of the high windows, looking down onto the street. Before he came over and greeted Jon and Rickard, he pulled the blue velvet draperies closed.

The boys stood as if ready to run. They couldn't help it. At any moment the doorbell might ring. The sound of swords and heavy steps would reach the vestibule, and the peaceful housekeeper would probably faint!

Though every passing second was precious, Rickard and Jon stood, silent, looking at the teacher. Their respect for him lingered on. They were used to replying only when addressed, and thus it was the teacher who had to begin the conversation.

"And what are my young pupils doing?"

"Well, I hoped—I thought I might come after my herbarium, if it's convenient for you," Rickard replied.

Mr. Ryd's pince-nez glasses glistened in the yellowish

light of the lamp. They saw the teacher's figure more or less as a shadow. But his face and his white hair looked very light against the blue velvet draperies.

It was quiet in the room. The heavy curtains helped to muffle noises from the outside. They could still hear faint signs of life, sounds from the riot down on the street. Was it the neighing of the horses? Was it human screams? Was there another shot? It was hard to make out. The sounds had melted into unreality.

Jon felt as if he wanted to look through the blue draperies that hid the windows. He could still feel perspiration running down his back.

The draperies told him nothing.

But at that very moment, in a fleeting second, Rickard's rough hand grabbed him by the wrist. Jon looked at the hand. The dizziness left him. There was Rickard's jacket sleeve with one button hanging loose, there were his chin, his rounded forehead, and below it his deep-set gray eyes. They observed Jon tensely; they were disturbed, not over what was going on outside, but over him, Jon.

A sense of certainty grew in him. Here was something to hang onto in the midst of the tumult—Rickard's world and his own. The destinies that awaited them were united. That was right. It was real. It would help both of them to live their lives.

The teacher spoke.

"Just a little while ago," he said, "I stood at my window and watched. I saw people assembling; I saw blue banners, yellow banners, and red banners. I saw the custodians of law and order appear, and I saw the police cordon. It occurred to me that the world was on the threshold of great changes and that it was right and proper that some young people were out there in the midst of it."

For a moment he stopped, and it seemed that he, too, might be listening. But inside they couldn't hear a sound.

"I don't know if all that violence was necessary. Certainly, it was unwise to throw burning torches and smoke bombs at the constables, who were only doing their duty."

The teacher had stepped over near the table. He took his rolled-up red handkerchief and weighed it in his hand.

"I noticed," he continued, "that my pupils were fleeing the scene. Ah, well, better to flee than to struggle.

"I don't believe either of my pupils were engaged in any of the evil deeds against the police."

Rickard stepped up to the table.

"We went there just to find out what the young socialists have in mind," he said. "If you don't take the trouble to find out and then do something . . ."

Jon was still perspiring. His forehead was dripping wet.

"We just want to find out . . ." he said.

At that moment the doorbell rang. All three of them heard it. The teacher placed his handkerchief on the felt cloth. With measured and dignified steps, he walked toward the door and pressed the light switch. The bronze ceiling lamp, many-armed, with pastel fabric shades covering the bulbs, shed light all over the room. The teacher returned to his desk, where the stacks of herbariums lay. The covers were brown and green, the pages white, and the protective covers yellow.

The silence was broken by booming bass voices from the vestibule.

"Let's have some light," the teacher said. "Let all of our actions be illuminated."

Lifting up several small herbariums, he pulled one of the thickest from the pile.

"Here," he continued, straightening his glasses, "here is young Mr. Svensson's herbarium. The drudgery of the previous summer . . ."

Leaning over the desk, he lowered his voice.

"I can well understand that my pupils had some important experiences during the summer vacation. It is right of my pupils to follow up these experiences. I trust that this is being done with sense and intelligence."

There was a knock at the door. From the opening you could hear the rustle of the housekeeper's voluminous skirts.

The teacher raised his voice.

"This collection is a fine demonstration of the knowledge acquired by young Mr. Svensson some time ago. Some of these examples are worthy of very high praise. . . . Yes, who is it, Mrs. Burk?"

The housekeeper had truly been frightened out of her wits. Red in the face, she was wringing her hands.

"Mr. Ryd, Mr. Ryd, the police! They're outside, and they say . . ."

The teacher leaned his hands against the table.

"Mrs. Burk, please calm yourself. There are no breakers of the law here. I will talk with them."

With one hand he gestured to the boys, inviting them to sit on the sofa, but they remained standing. Then, with measured steps, he walked to the vestibule. He left the door behind him half open so that the boys, no longer in the realm of fantasy but in the midst of grim reality, heard the rattle of the swords. They also heard the click of boots in a military salute. The voices of the constables were vague and rumbling, but the voice of their teacher came through distinctly and clearly. They heard every word.

"Both of the boys are pupils of mine in the Soltuna Consolidated Latin School. They were on their way here to pick up their herbariums. . . . No trouble at all. . . . These riots are unpleasant, to be sure, but their roots are in certain civic conditions. . . . One regrets the fact that innocent people are involved. The discussions should take place in parliamentary order, in the government, not on the streets and in the public squares. . . . Gentlemen, no reason. No reason at all."

The vestibule door closed again. The housekeeper let out a stream of terrified complaints. It was she who first appeared at the workroom door.

"My dear boys!" she said. "I'm going to get you a couple of glasses of currant juice. I thought you looked completely flustered when you came!"

The skirts rustled away.

When the teacher returned to his workroom, Rickard and Jon were still glued to the same place as before. They wanted to say something but didn't quite know what.

Their teacher stood before them. For a few seconds he seemed very far away. It looked almost as though he were trying to peer through the blue draperies out onto the street. Then, smiling behind his pince-nez glasses, he lifted his hand and patted each of them on the shoulder, first Rickard, then Jon. The gesture was slow and ceremonious.

The boys again bowed.

Once more silence reigned in the room. Then Mr. Ryd walked over to his desk. Taking off his glasses, he breathed on them and polished them. His nearsighted eyes were filled with kindness.

"While we wait for the juice," he said as he began to untie the ribbon on Rickard's plant collection, "while we wait for the juice, which the kind Mrs. Burk is going to serve us, I think we ought to refresh our memories with a glance at young Mr. Svensson's well-pressed examples of *Pyrola umbellata*.

"Then I would like to hear more about the little fellow—what was his name?—oh, yes, little Pelle from Ulvahult."